MW01598402

Corridors

By Michael Galloway

© 2013 by Michael Galloway. All rights reserved. Cover illustration by Shoosashi, Valerie Larson, and Michael Galloway.

ISBN-13: 978-0-9847402-4-6

No part of this book may be reproduced, stored in a retrieval system, or transmitted by any means, electronic, mechanical, photocopying, recording or otherwise without written permission from the author.

www.michaelgalloway.net

The short stories in this collection are works of fiction. Names, characters, places, and events are products of the author's imagination or are used fictitiously. Any resemblance to actual persons, living or dead, locations or events is entirely coincidental.

Contents

Firebugs

Dr. Ferganut sat hunched over on a wooden barstool and fiddled with a tiny metallic sculpture that looked more like a child's toy than a feat of micro engineering. To him it was the crown of his creations, ready for its first long range test flight over the wilderness. With a wingspan that could fit in the palm of his hand and a shape like a dragonfly, his wirefly was ready to change the world of aviation forever. After a swarm of failures, false starts, and flawed flight paths, he knew today would be transformational.

He picked up the metallic insect and walked outside of his cabin laboratory. The smell of forest fire smoke hung in the air as the hazy afternoon sun struggled to shine through. He set the shiny silver-and-cobalt blue machine onto the brown, wooden picnic table in his front yard. The pines swayed in the breeze around him but the crunch of dry, brown pine needles underfoot reminded him at every step that the forest around him was drowning in drought and ready to kindle in an instant.

He clicked the on button on the hand held remote control. With a flip of the switch and at the twist of a black knob, the wirefly was airborne.

The insect machine hovered over the table a moment, undisturbed by the acrid breeze, and then lifted higher and higher until it was barely visible above the crown of the pines. With a whirr of wings it zipped over the trees and off to the northwest, carrying a tiny camera that beamed back black-and-white images every few seconds.

Dr. Ferganut smiled to himself and stepped back inside. He sat down on the bar stool again and stared at his laptop, which was connected by a long cable to a fifteen-foot antenna in his backyard. The data streaming back from the wirefly was marvelous as it soared above the trees and followed the Gunflint Trail northwest towards the Canadian border. In hours the real answers would come as the device made a one-hundred mile arc around the region and circled back home.

* * *

A half hour later he drove to the Northeaster Lodge and General Store further south along the Gunflint Trail and stepped inside. Deena, the clerk behind the counter, waved to him and he returned a triumphant grin. His elated mood soon crashed like a broken kite. In a back corner of the store, amidst all the shelves and racks bursting with hats, sweatshirts, books, and stuffed animals, a black-haired man shuffled through a stack of tee shirts. From the side, it looked like an old fellow engineering classmate of his from his days at Rensselaer, except for the black ponytail running down to the middle of the back. The man wore a black leather jacket and held a black motorcycle helmet under one arm.

Dr. Ferganut strode over to him and picked up a loaf of bread from a nearby shelf. "Dr. Minton? Is that you?"

The man turned towards him and in an instant they recognized each other. Dr. Minton stared coldly at him at first. After a delay, he smiled. "What are you doing here, Jim?"

"I was going to ask you the same question. I live up here in the summer. What have you been up to?"

"A little...research. Maybe with a bit of recreation thrown in." There was a cool, unsettling darkness in his eyes as they drifted to another shelf and then back towards Dr. Ferganut.

"Do have you time for some coffee?"

"I can't stand coffee. Or have you forgotten?"

Dr. Ferganut backed up a step. "It's just a saying. I didn't mean anything by it."

"Oh, I know what you mean. Memory never was one of your strong points, was it? Good day, Jim."

Dr. Minton strode past him and left without another word. Dr. Ferganut turned to see him leave. Soon, the chug-chug-roar of a motorcycle filled the parking lot and then Minton was gone. He walked up to the counter.

"Do you know him?" Deena asked, drumming her black-and-green painted nails on the countertop. She was in her early twenties, and had long, straight, black hair with green streaks in it.

"Not anymore. Did he say where he was staying?"

"He didn't say a thing to me the whole time he was here."

Dr. Ferganut placed a loaf of cranberry bread on the counter, along with a couple cans of beef vegetable soup. He stared out the front window of the store.

She rang up his grocery items and read off the total. "Whoever he is, I've seen him around here on his bike the past couple of days. And I don't think he's out kayaking."

"No, he was never into nature much."

"So how do you know him again?"

"We went to school together. Then we had a falling out. He thought I stole his girlfriend or something like that."

"Did you?"

"No, but he stole mine. Funny how that works. We used to play board games once in a while and he would obsess over losses until he found out a way to beat you."

"Sounds like a walking time bomb."

"He's one guy that hates to lose."

"By the way, do you plan on sticking around tonight? DNR says the fire might come through here."

"Did they figure out how it started?"

"One says lightning. Another says a cigarette. If you ask me, I don't think it was either of those."

* * *

At four-thirty in the morning the laptop on the kitchen table sounded an alarm. Dr. Ferganut leapt out of bed and bounded into the kitchen. The display told him the wirefly was still in flight, but within a quarter mile of landing back on the picnic table out front. He threw on a pair of sweatpants and a tee shirt as fast as he could and ran outside with a flashlight and his laptop.

What should have been a vast canopy of stars above was replaced with a dome of smoke. Birds chirped away in the trees in anticipation of the sunrise but the orange glow to the south and now to the west was from anything but the sun. The air was still but the smoke smell was far worse than the night before.

He coughed and jogged down the dirt driveway to stand on the service road. Down about a mile he spied orange flames licking the treetops and a shower of embers hitting the road. He dashed back into his cabin and began to box up his notes and equipment. He had prepared for this day and although it made him sad, he would know in minutes if the flight plan worked. Nothing, not even fire, could steal that triumph away.

After boxing up his papers and electronics, he filled the trunk and the back seat of his car. In the distance above the symphony of bird calls, he heard the high pitched whirr of the metallic cicada. He scampered back to the picnic table and stared at his laptop screen. Fifty feet. Forty feet. Thirty...

In seconds, the wirefly descended onto the table. The wings of the device stilled and in jubilation he scooped it up and held it up to the sky. He shook his fist in the direction of the blaze and then picked up his laptop.

He set the fly and the laptop on the passenger seat of his car and drove off. In his rearview mirror he saw the silhouette of his transmission tower left now to face an onslaught of combustion alone. His heart sank but he pressed on.

* * *

As he left the service road and drove onto the Gunflint Trail, he noticed the trees were alive with flames in several directions. Then, a tiny, green glow followed by a bright, white flash caught his eye along the roadside. He pulled over since it did not look like any firefly he ever knew about.

He stared around on the shoulder of the road a moment, but could not pinpoint the spot of the flash. It looked like the kind of flash he saw in science class once, unusually bright and...

Suddenly, a patch of ground before him ignited into flame. He drew back at first, then crouched down. There, in the growing flame, he saw the husk of a small, metallic object. He poured out a bottle of water he had been drinking onto the fire and snuffed it out. With a crooked stick he found on the shoulder he picked at the embers and the object.

He reached over and picked it up. Charred and malformed, he held the object up to his flashlight and found it had legs. Six of them. And a head. And a thorax. And wings.

He saw another green flash some fifty feet ahead. He carried the bug with him and jumped back into his car. Daybreak would come soon, but he knew it would only take him an hour or less to reverse engineer what he found.

* * *

He parked his car and bolted back into his cabin. He hauled out some of his equipment, his laptop, and a shoebox full of prototype wireflies he built over the previous months.

He set the charred insect shell onto the kitchen table and dissected it with a tweezers and a magnifying glass. The work seemed familiar, yet evolved somehow. The electronics were melted beyond recognition, but the design reminded him of a drawing he had seen a decade earlier.

Suddenly, it all fell into place. He opened his laptop computer and plugged the cable into the antenna system. With lightning-quick movements, his fingers pounded out a new set of instructions for his box of prototype wireflies. The whole box of them—fifty test models in all—would be sent on one-way missions into the depths of the surrounding forest.

After finishing the new instructions, he turned each insect on and carried the box outside. He set them all up on the picnic table one by one, lining them up like planes on a gigantic aircraft carrier. One after another they took flight, each one programmed to dive bomb the green-and-white glowing metallic bugs, pick them up, and carry them into the air where they would explode harmlessly. If they did not ignite, each wirefly would home in on the fire station in Grand Marais and land in the parking lot. After the last bug took flight he ran back into the cabin, unplugged his equipment and drove off down the road.

At six in the morning he put a call into the local fire station. "I think I figured something out," he told the fire chief. "These fires weren't started by lightning. Keep an eye on the sky. You should be getting a visitor or two soon. But the name of the guy you want goes by the name of Dr. Minton."

Dr. Ferganut hung up his cell phone and sat on the shoulder of the road, watching the incoming data on his laptop. The system was working off of a weaker mobile antenna set up in the trunk of his car, but for now if would suffice. Some of the video showed the green-glowing bugs on the forest floor, followed by a swift dive towards the ground, and then nothing as both were incinerated in midair.

Perhaps this would go on for hours, but he was a patient man, especially when it came to Dr. Minton. After all, they had a game to finish.

The Bells of Copernicus

The lightning lit up the clouds below like fireflies trapped in cobwebs. In between the thunderheads were the outlines of continents and on those continents orange and white-lit cities dotted the land like electrified spiders. As the moon shuttle began its descent towards the Earth's atmosphere, Croix leaned back in his seat and took in the view. When viewed from space, the cities of Earth seemed more alive than the domed cities of the Moon.

The passenger in the seat next to him stopped flipping through his magazine and looked up. "So you say you helped build a shrine? That's amazing. What did the architect use for wall materials? Mooncrete or something imported?"

"The walls were brick, but the foundation was made of moon rock."

"Really? Sounds like what we did with the project I was on. Did they by chance happen to use the melted rock from the Copernicus crater?"

"Sure did. Strange stuff to work with."

"As I recall, they did that with a church in Germany. They used some rock from a nearby crater. It's beautiful material. How did they construct the roof?"

"Part steel, part Mooncrete." Croix looked out the window again and watched as the hull of their shuttle began to glow orange.

"Now entering Earth's atmosphere," came an automated female voice over the intercom system.

The passenger next to Croix extended a hand to shake. "My name's Phil, by the way. I'm the architect on the new cathedral going up in New Copernicus."

"Nice to meet you. I'm Croix. About your cathedral. How tall is it?"

"Only a couple stories. Although you can see the spire from

anywhere inside the dome. We imported all the windows, though."

"Stained glass windows?"

"Yes. They were shipped up here all the way from the States. I wish they'd figure out how to manufacture it up here."

Croix watched as the orange reentry glow obscured the view out of the window and bathed the passenger compartment in a bright orange light. Some passengers shut the sliding shield over their windows while Croix and Phil slipped on the sunglasses the shuttle service provided.

Phil continued. "So tell me something else about this shrine you worked on. Does it have pews? The one I designed had handcrafted wooden ones."

"No, no pews. There's a bench. And some metal stools, too."

"Sounds more like a bar than a shrine. How about bells? Does it have those? I thought we sounded the first church bells in any domed city on the Moon."

"No, no bells. Well, maybe now that I think about it. But no bell tower. Hey were you testing your church's bells the other day? I thought I heard them through the walls. Come to think of it, there's a window with a view of your church."

Phil held a puzzled look on his face. "We were. Funny, I didn't realize they were building two churches so close together. What religion did you say your shrine was for?"

"Oh, it's not for a religion. It's an arcade."

"An arcade? Like part of a mall?"

"No. Like a coin-op arcade without the coins. The developer is doing it for some guy who's on his way up here from Earth. Guess the guy wants to live up here or something. Bring his kids and grandkids and all that."

"But you said it was a shrine."

Croix let out a big smile. "I did. It's got all the great ones in it: Pac-Man, Centipede, Mario Brothers, and even Marble Madness." He laughed but Phil kept a straight-ahead, dead-serious look. "Yeah, Mr. Stonehill is kind of an odd guy."

"Stonehill you say? What's his first name?"

"Edmund."

"Reverend Edmund Stonehill?"

"Maybe. Come to think of it, he was wearing a collar when I first

11

met with him."

Image Management

Dell leaned forward over his desk and stared at the computer screen in disbelief. He cradled the telephone receiver with his shoulder and typed the query request again.

"I'm telling you, this morning the images were there, Mrs. Fenton," he said.

Mrs. Fenton continued yelling in his ear.

"We do have backup systems. Lots of failsafes."

More chatter.

"Yes, we know what we're doing. We'll keep looking into it. Good day, Mrs. Fenton."

Dell slammed down the receiver and rubbed his temples with his fingers. "Becky, I need your assistance."

A redheaded woman with curly hair approached from the reception area. She was ten years his junior but would probably go ten times farther if given the chance. She handed him a clipboard full of papers. "Aren't you glad you hired me?" She said with a grin.

Dell grabbed the clipboard. He set it on his desk and then flicked through the papers. Just like Mrs. Fenton's husband, there had to be a dozen other examples of memory storage corruption on some level.

"When was the first time you noticed this happening?" He asked Becky, not looking up.

"Yesterday afternoon was the first I heard of it. Mrs. Luck called up saying her husband couldn't remember their family dog after his visit yesterday."

Dell closed his eyes and tried to dream of his last vacation to Mexico. The only image that came into his mind was that of a traffic jam at the border crossing. He looked up and picked up the phone again. "I need Jamie from IT over here right away. He's gonna ask for a pay raise after he sees this mess."

Dell looked back at Becky. "Thanks."

"Any idea what happened?"

"All we have to go on is that sometime yesterday, probably around the time Mr. Luck came in, something got corrupted in our image database servers. From what I'm seeing whole memories are being dropped. Even with new clients. But when the old clients come in and get some of their old memories reloaded, a bunch of images are missing. The missing dog memories are just the beginning."

"Should we close or should I work on my resume?"

"Lock the doors. Cross-check everybody that calls and whatever you do, don't take any new appointments this afternoon."

* * *

Dell and Jamie spent the rest of the afternoon digging through the database. Dell continued to flip through the stored memory images on his computer screen at lightning speed. "It's really creepy looking at some of the memories people store here. Sometimes I wish I hadn't looked."

A knock came at the door. The door opened.

"Dell, Mr. Luck is here again," Becky said, looking worried.

"Tell him we're closed."

"I did. He won't leave. Every time I close the blinds on one window he goes to the next one. Will you come out here and talk to him?"

Dell grunted and stood up. He followed Becky back to the reception area. Mr. Luck stood in front of the curved, oak and glass reception desk, fiddling with his brown hat and whistling to himself.

Dell extended a hand to Mr. Luck. "Mr. Luck, what can I do for you?"

Mr. Luck put his hat back onto his head. "You can fix what you screwed up yesterday. How about that?"

"What seems to be the problem?"

"Don't you talk to your staff? I'll tell you what's wrong. I came in here to get some memories offloaded for storage and get some old ones put back in so I can go on a cruise with my wife and you botched it up." He stuck his finger into Dell's chest. "I come home and I don't recognize my dog. Had that fool thing fifteen years my wife said. Didn't recognize my garden. Said to my wife, who planted carrots?"

14

"Okay. Let me take a look at your file."

"You better take a look. Get me back in your office now before I sue. I'll have my lawyer on your case before you can say litigation."

Dell frowned at Becky. Becky mouthed the word "litigation" and smiled at Mr. Luck. Dell then led Mr. Luck back into the examination room and directed him to sit in the patient chair. The chair was covered in brown vinyl and above the chair was a mechanical arm that had a clear helmet with silver electrodes around it. A spaghetti tangle of canary yellow wires ran down from the helmet and along the length of the mechanical arm.

Dell fired up the exam computer and brought up Mr. Luck's file onscreen. He stared at the screen a minute.

"Well? What does it say? Where's my dog? And what happened to my love of gardening?" Mr. Luck chided. His hands clenched the chair's armrests hard enough to tear them apart.

"Says here you saw Dr. Glazer."

"That's right, I saw Dr. Glazer. Maybe you should call him."

"It's his day off."

"I don't care if it's his day off. I want my memories back."

Dell gripped a pen between his teeth hard enough to snap it in half. The system told him Mr. Luck came in to have some work-related memories removed. Nothing else. No dogs, no gardens…

"Where do you work, Mr. Luck?"

"I'm a plumber. I can't believe how many times I've been asked that question today. Don't you people talk to each other?" Mr. Luck reached up and grabbed the helmet with both hands. "Here. Let's get this done. I have a plane to catch."

Dell reached over to stop the helmet from coming down. "Mr. Luck, please. In a minute. Says here you came to have your work memories for the past six months offloaded to storage. We did that. Looks like you come here every six months. It's happened for years now."

"I'm a loyal customer, that's why. Until now. Just fix what you screwed up and then I'm outta here."

"Okay." Dell flipped through the offloaded images from yesterday and found pictures of Mr. Luck's golden retriever walking into the garden, pawing at the dirt, and tearing up the plants. In the images, he could also see they were from the perspective of the inside of a truck, with paperwork on the dashboard.

"Do you drive a truck, Mr. Luck?"

"It's not a truck, it's a van. I use it for work."

Dell could see another image of the approach to the garden, which was next to the driveway. Then, another image of the dog running off. Then, another of the garden with the plants and their roots torn asunder. Lastly, he saw a broken carrot top laying next to the green chicken wire fence running around the perimeter of the garden.

"What's taking so long?" Mr. Luck whined. "What are you looking at?"

"Do you think about your garden much? How about your dog?"

"Oh, how would I know. I didn't know I had a dog or a garden until my wife reminded me."

Dell set up the machine to reload the dog and garden images. After the processing was completed, he leaned over to lower the helmet over Mr. Luck's head. "Close your eyes, Mr. Luck. This will only take a minute."

Mr. Luck complied as Dell fired up the machine. The helmet lit up like a neon beer sign and Mr. Luck heaved a sigh.

The machine whirred to life for a minute and then fell silent. Dell read the message off the screen: "Download complete." He turned to Mr. Luck. "You should now have your dog and your garden back."

He lifted the helmet off of Mr. Luck's head. Mr. Luck opened his eyes but stared straight ahead for a minute before turning towards him.

"Well?" Dell asked. "Do you remember your dog's name now? Do you remember what's in your garden?"

Mr. Luck heaved another sigh. "You didn't put any of my work memories back, right? Mrs. Luck won't have any of that on our trip. She's the reason I'm here after all."

"What about your dog? Remember his name?"

"It's a female, and her name is Bandit. And in my garden there are carrots, tomatoes, strawberries, and rhubarb."

His voice trailed off.

"What?"

"I said to get rid of my work memories."

"We did. I only put the dog memories and the garden back."

"No, no. Oh no. No." Mr. Luck leaned back and clenched his fists again. "Take the box, then. Take the box!"

"Box? What box?"

"The box in the garden. There's a metal box in the garden. It's got my winnings in it. I can't have that come up on this trip. It'll be the end of me. You've got to help me, doc. Take the box. I'll find it again, I will."

"Why do you have a box buried in your garden?"

"If she finds the box she'll kill me. Please, doc, take the box."

Dell turned back to the computer screen. He skimmed through Mr. Luck's profile again. He did not see any red flags. "When you first saw us, Mr. Luck, did you tell us about this?"

"What? The box?"

"No. Your...gambling habits."

"Oh, I only do it a little on the side. Now and then."

"Like every day?"

"What's wrong with a little bet now and then?"

Dell closed his eyes and had no idea what to do next. Screening, after all, was supposed to eliminate the risky ones: schizophrenics, addicts, Alzheimer patients, gamblers, and others with criminal histories. "The problem is that you probably had been thinking about the box all day. Am I right?"

Mr. Luck gave a sheepish grin.

"Now those memories are tied to your garden and your dog. When did the dog dig up the garden?"

"A week ago. Doc, just fix the box and I'll be on my way."

Dell flipped through some images of boxes that Mr. Luck offloaded. "What kind of box was it?"

"A metal one. About the size of a shoebox. It's copper-colored and has a black handle on the cover. It was my wife's old jewelry box. She used it up until the day we were married."

"Okay. I'll take the box. This is risky, though."

"Not as risky if you leave it in there!"

Dell lowered the helmet again and fired up the machine. Again, the contraption lit up like a neon beer sign and whirred like a vacuum cleaner. After the procedure was complete, he lifted the helmet off of his client's head.

Mr. Luck sat up in the chair for the first time since he arrived and smiled. He put his hands on his knees and then picked up his hat off the nearby work desk. "Much better. See you in six months."

"What about the box in your garden?"

"What box?"

Dell smiled in relief. "Just a trick question to see if everything worked properly."

"Ah. All is well."

"Have a safe trip with your wife."

Mr. Luck reached for the door and put his hand on the doorknob. He stopped and turned back to face Dell. "Who?"

A Fifth of Amber

Every night Dalton would make the trek down the block to read the light-up display on the edge of downtown and every night he would return empty-handed, still holding the beige ticket stub in his hands like a rare coin. The numbers were still legible on the ticket despite him putting it inside a plastic sandwich bag and stuffing the bag in his shoe before going to bed each night.

Bed, of course, was either an alley or a beat-up mattress under a highway overpass or maybe even a park bench. In winter, bed meant the local homeless shelter. Tonight it was a park bench, he decided, after staring up at the giant illuminated sign, which had a ticker for news, information, but more important, the week's poverty lottery winners.

On his journey back towards the bench in Rice Park, he heard a man shouting up ahead of him on the street. Dalton stuffed his hands into his pockets and winced. He knew the sound because it had been burned into his mind a thousand times: yet another lottery winner would jump for joy and get their chance to move to a different sector of the city or use their ticket to buy an option grant. Most chose freedom, which came in the form of a new job, home, and perhaps the chance to be reunited with their families in the working class sector.

The man approached Dalton, running, and carrying a suitcase full of belongings. He came up to Dalton, but Dalton could barely recall the man's name. He had seen him working as a street sweeper before. The man had brown, shoulder-length hair, stood at over six and a half feet tall and was skinnier than a street lamp post.

He grabbed Dalton's shirt by the arms while still holding the suitcase and almost knocked Dalton to the ground with his enthusiasm. "I did it. My number was picked."

An instant later he let go and ran off. He stopped a moment and turned back. "Just you wait, Dalton. You're next. I'll put in a good word for you."

Dalton faked a smile but knew it was all garbage talk. No one ever came back for anyone else, no one sent letters, and no one called. Dalton read enough to know that there was no communication between the government-created sectors, except by the authorities or the government services people themselves. Even then it was only to inform you of a relative passing away. Besides, the man reeked of vodka so who knew if he was telling the truth anyway.

He continued on towards the park and in the distance he could see the outer rim wall. The top of it was lit up like a set of runway lights, except no planes would land and help one fly away. He wondered if planes still flew in the affluent sector as he had not heard a plane engine in years.

In minutes he found his usual park bench, unoccupied and quiet in the tree-shrouded corner of the park. The nearby oak and maple trees radiated the heat now that they had absorbed all day long from the sun. He withdrew a pair of jeans from his backpack. He rolled the jeans into a pillow, propped it under his head, and stretched out his weary legs. He stared up at the night sky, eyeing the belt of Orion. In minutes, he closed his eyes and dreamt of the planes he used to fly for a living.

* * *

The following morning he awoke to the sound of a police siren that zipped past the park, followed by an ambulance. He sat up, rubbed his eyes, and looked at the ground around him. A gray and white pigeon pecked at the sidewalk before him.

He checked his watch. It was the first of June, which meant only one thing: Release Day. He stood up, brushed off his blue denim shirt and picked up his backpack. He stuffed the jeans inside his backpack and walked towards the downtown billboard.

In minutes he came upon the billboard and looked up to see a vast array of numbers. There were so many numbers that his imagination began to run all the digits together. His heart leapt a moment, however, when a sequence that perhaps matched his own ticket appeared in the far right corner of the board.

In his excitement, he knelt down, untied his shoe and pulled out the sandwich bag. He held up the ticket towards the sign and checked it against the billboard seven times. Every digit matched.

A block from the billboard up ahead two lines already formed. Each one was one hundred people long apiece. They stood waiting in front of the work authorization building whose two temporary windows were now open. The building was two stories tall and made of featureless crimson brick. The windows were shiny, black, and opaque. He dashed up to the back of the line to the right which appeared to be the shorter of the two.

He clenched his ticket tight, then thought better of it and placed it back inside his plastic bag and shoved it into his front pants pocket. He clutched his backpack tight after hearing some commotion behind him.

"Take the amber," a man shouted out from behind. "Best option up there."

Dalton turned around to see a black-and-gray haired man in his fifties counseling others behind him. He turned back before he got counseled himself. The line inched forward.

"Ninety slots remain for travel to the next sector," said a female voice over the work authorization building loudspeaker. A couple of groans and shouts came from behind him.

"Save a spot for us," cried a woman in her forties in the other line, shaking her fist at those in front of her. More counseling came from the man behind him.

The last thing Dalton wanted was a fifth of amber. He had heard many a horror story about the substance, from men going insane due to its contents, to others staying drunk for what seemed like weeks, to others who had died hours later. In half the cases there appeared to be an increase in intelligence, which, so the theory went, was supposed to help one move up in work rank with the hopes of being promoted out of the sector entirely. Dalton could not think of anyone who had been promoted this way, but still the rumors persisted on the streets.

The man behind Dalton tapped him on the shoulder. "You're taking the amber, right?"

Dalton turned to look back.

The loudspeaker bellowed out again, "Seventy slots remaining."

"You hear that?" The man said. He jabbed his index finger into Dalton's jacket. "Seventy. Do us a favor. Take the amber."

"I'll think about it," Dalton replied, turning back.

He felt a hand on his shoulder now, pulling him back around.

"No. Take it, my friend."

The line crept forward. Dalton counted off fifty people in front of him in his line alone, which meant dwindling odds and dwindling choices by the time he would arrive at the front of the line. His shoulders tensed up.

The man in front of him turned around. "Can you believe him?"

"Not really."

"What are you taking?"

"I don't know yet. It depends on…"

"He's taking the fifth of amber like I told 'em to," said a voice from behind him again. Dalton noticed that the man reeked of cheap beer and urine and was holding a beige ticket in his hand.

The line moved forward again, much faster now, as Dalton watched another freedom card get handed out, and several workers taking a set of light blue work clothes, which meant a status upgrade.

"Twenty-five freedom slots remain," boomed the loudspeaker again.

Dalton counted off the workers in front of him. There were now twenty in front of him, and the line to the left moved slower. He turned back towards the man behind him. "A fifth of amber, eh?"

"That's right. If you know what's good for you."

"Have you taken it before?"

"I have. It's worth a fortune on the streets." The man pointed at his own chest. "Take it from a man of taste like me."

Dalton peered down at the sidewalk then back up at the man. "Can I see your winning ticket?"

The man held it out for Dalton to see, but drew it back after a few seconds.

Dalton nodded and smiled, having memorized the sequence of numbers. He gazed over at another, smaller, lit-up billboard which listed the winning numbers. He scanned the list twice, but the closest match he found was one number off. A wry smile broke across his face as the line surged forward.

Soon, he found himself nearly at the front of the line. The adjacent line struggled to move forward. From a distance, it looked like a paperwork mix-up with one of the workers. Some workers in the other line began to complain and argue.

Dalton felt another tap on the shoulder. He turned around and braced himself for a fight.

"Take the amber. I know where you eat. I know where you sleep."

Dalton approached the window attendant. She had long blonde hair wound up into a bun and wore a sharp, creased, midnight blue uniform. Her face was expressionless.

"Let's see your ticket," she said and held out a hand towards Dalton.

"In a moment. I want this man to go first." Dalton stepped aside and let the man behind him move up.

"Wise man, wise man," the man said.

The clerk's eyes widened as the man stepped forward. Dalton dropped back behind him and waited.

The man handed the clerk his beige ticket and cleared his throat. "I'll take my freedom card now."

The clerk examined the ticket and shook her head. She held it up to her computer monitor. Her eyes darted back and forth. "This ticket's no good. Please step out of the line."

The man cursed and slammed his fist onto the counter. Two security officers dressed in black uniforms with red stripes on their shoulders swooped in and escorted him away a moment later. In seconds all three were on the ground wrestling until the officers regained control.

The clerk then motioned for Dalton to step forward. On the window ledge were three objects: a square, orange card the size of a playing card, a neatly folded light-blue uniform with a pale blue card on top of it, and a rectangular glass flask with a cork and amber liquid inside of it.

Dalton read the multitude of stories about the liquid from it being liquefied tree resin to plain whiskey to it being some type of interstellar elixir. His eyes locked onto the bottle, then drifted away.

"Well?" The clerk pressed, impatient.

Dalton pointed to the leftmost object. "I'll take the freedom card."

The clerk finally showed the first hint of emotion. Her soft green eyes connected with his, if only for a moment. "Wise man. It was the last one for the year."

Consider the Ant

Dr. Gates scooped sand out of the white, five-gallon plastic bucket on the floor and into the terrarium. After several scoops, he turned to his colleague, Dr. Bell. "How full do you want this?"

"To within four inches of the top."

"At this rate, I'll be here the rest of the night."

"Let me give you a hand with that."

Dr. Bell helped Dr. Gates dump the whole bucket of sand into the glass tank. Then they picked up two more buckets and emptied them into the tank.

Dr. Gates smoothed out the top of the sand pile with the palm of his hand. "Ready with the ants?"

"Ready with the lid?"

Dr. Bell turned back towards a shoebox-sized, clear plastic box on the counter. Inside were four hundred metallic ants, the size of carpenter ants, climbing and tumbling all over each other in a writhing mass. From a distance, it looked as if a puddle of mercury had come to life.

He walked back towards the terrarium with the plastic box of ants cradled under his arm. A nervous excitement spread throughout his body as if the butterflies in his stomach suddenly became electrified.

He held one hand on the bottom of the box and the other on the lid, and dumped the contents into the terrarium. Dr. Gates then slid the terrarium lid into place.

Dr. Bell sprinted over to the digital video camera mounted on a tripod in the middle of the lab floor. After a few adjustments, he pressed the record button and stepped back towards the terrarium.

At first, the ants remained in a tangled heap, each one crawling on top of the other as if somehow disorientated yet clinging to each other. One by one the ants dropped off the pile and onto the sand, at first sinking down then tunneling their way back to daylight.

The two scientists stood back and watched for several minutes in silence. The metallic ants continued to fan out across the top of the sand pile and after a few minutes a handful of them began to burrow down below the surface.

Dr. Bell turned towards his colleague. "Do you really trust that lid to hold tonight?"

"Don't you trust your own programming?"

"Well, yeah, but like any piece of software there's bound to be bugs that only pop up when it gets field tested."

Dr. Bell watched in fascination as the mass of silver little creatures untangled themselves and went to work building a giant anthill. For all the computer simulations he watched over the past six months, none of them seemed to compare to the actions of the real models at work. Yet there was one variable that concerned him: food.

He picked up a Hershey's chocolate bar off of his desk and unwrapped the bar halfway. He broke off a rectangular chunk and ate it. "What do you think they'll do instead of storing up food?"

"Didn't you account for that in your calculations?"

"Certainly. I prioritized survival first, then social order, and then exploration." Dr. Bell then broke off another piece of chocolate.

After a few more minutes of notes and observations, Dr. Gates turned to watch his computer screen and then picked up his coat off the back of his black swivel chair. "I'm off. Don't have too much fun."

Dr. Bell waved him off and continued to watch the ants tunnel their way through the sand at an astounding rate, and much faster than any ants he remembered from the sidewalks of his childhood. A few of the ants managed to pile up in the corner of the tank, as if they were building their own Tower of Babel.

He set his half-eaten chocolate bar still in its wrapper onto his desk. Next to his computer monitor was a watercolor painting of his family created by his daughter Megan. He loved the painting because of the obvious love she put into it. He committed himself to hanging it on the wall tomorrow morning. At that he picked up his coat and left for the night.

* * *

In the morning, Dr. Bell arrived alone to find the top of the terrarium still intact. New tunnels had been built in the sand, but except for a couple stray ants the tank was empty. He then checked the lid, but found it still in place.

Suddenly, he felt a stinging pain on his right hand. He looked to find one of the ants crawling up his ring finger and then along the back of his hand. He carried it over to the plastic holding box, dropped it inside, and secured the lid.

Worried, he searched around the nearby tables but found no signs of the other ants. He checked the top of the terrarium again and found a pencil-sized hole had been chewed through the plastic. His eye then caught sight of a lone ant, most likely a scout, bumbling its way across the tabletop and towards the wall.

Dr. Bell then pulled out a black light flashlight and shone it on the tabletop. Tiny dotted chemical trails could be seen up and down the walls of the tank, along the tabletop, and along the back wall. He shone the light along the wall and down to the floor where the trail led to a crack in the floor near an electrical outlet.

He dug into his jacket and pulled out his cell phone. After a minute, Dr. Gates' voice mail answered.

"You've got to get down here. They tunneled their way out of the tank."

He scanned around the floor but could not find any other trails. His mind raced with thoughts of where the creatures went next. He ran over to the wall behind the tank and put his ear up against it. Inside, he heard a rustling noise, which was followed by the lights flickering in the lab room.

On the adjacent wall opposite the door, the wall clock popped free from its hook and crashed to the floor. A dozen ants poured out of the hole in the wall where the clock hook once was as the lights in the room continued to flicker.

He ran over to the video camera and then to his computer terminal. After waking up his computer from its slumber, he brought up the video recording application. He rewound the video to a few hours earlier. Eventually he found the time that the ants burrowed out of the tank: four hours ago. By now, he figured, they were spread throughout the walls.

The few ants that clung to the wall clock now scurried their way across the floor. Other ants seemed to drip to the floor like pooling liquid metal. Dr. Bell smelled smoke and at once the lights went out for good.

He scrambled around for a regular flashlight but found none. He could hear the scurrying of tiny metallic feet across the cold, tiled floor as the odor of electrical smoke became overwhelming.

Fumbling along the tables, he lunged for the door. He was jolted backwards by the sting of tiny creatures on the doorknob and flicked them to the floor. The smell of smoke soon overpowered him as the fire alarm blasted to life. He covered his ears as the alarm light lit up the room with a faint white glow. The fire sprinklers jetted to life and doused everything in sight. Dr. Bell pounded on the door. He hollered. Finally, he found a loose rag on one of the work benches. Wrapping his hand in the rag he reached for the door handle and flung the door open to an equally dark hallway.

Moments later a loud crackling sound erupted from the lab. A bright flash of light lit up the room and the hallway as Dr. Bell staggered against a wall. The sound of sprinklers continued as water flowed out onto the hallway carpeting. Smoke poured out of the room as he darted for the front door of the building.

* * *

After the power had been cut to the building and the fire extinguished, Dr. Bell and Dr. Gates returned to the burned out shell of their lab. All their equipment and notes were charred, drenched, or smelled of smoke.

On the floor Dr. Bell noticed a blackened mass that looked more like a giant tangle of steel wool than a pile of ants. The ants had clung to each other into a floating mat, but also perished together.

"Electrocuted?" Dr. Bell asked.

Dr. Gates prodded at the mass with an angry stick. "Beyond recognition."

"Told you there'd be bugs."

"Dead ones?"

Dr. Bell continued to pace around the room in search of burned-out carcasses. Finding none, he looked over to the wall where the clock crashed only hours before. He then spied movement out of the corner of his eye near the muddied remains of the terrarium.

Dr. Gates looked over at him. "What is it?"

Dr. Bell walked over to the tank and watched as one of the metallic ants crawled out onto the table. He picked up a nearby log book and slammed it down with a bang onto the creature, disabling it. He held up the book and turned it over. The smashed shell of the ant clung to the book just like the real thing.

"Was that necessary?" Dr. Gates scolded.

Dr. Bell looked over at the other lab table and his wrecked computer. Next to his flooded keyboard was the half-eaten candy bar from last night. It was wet, but otherwise undisturbed.

Then he saw his daughter's watercolor painting drenched but also torn to pieces, as if the ants had rampaged over it first. He walked over to the painting and picked up the pieces. They fell between his fingertips like raindrops.

Dr. Gates clapped his hands together excitedly. "I just can't *wait* to see what you got planned for version 2.0."

Bridges to Eden

Cray sat on the floor and wiped the sweat from his brow. He wanted to throw his toolset into the great geared abyss below but thought better of it. Part of him wondered if throwing his tools over the railing would indeed wreak havoc with not only the printing presses but with the motions of the nearby planets as if some great celestial grandfather clock had blown out a cog. After all, he had been told before his arrival on this planet that he would get a glimpse of the inner workings of the universe despite being on probation.

"Giving up already?" A voice said from behind him.

Cray stood up and spun around, his brown cloak nearly getting caught up under one of his sandals. "I can't get this last cog in place on assembly twelve." He looked first at the grated floor, then up at his elder, Stanwick, who stood before him with his hood off.

Stanwick placed both of his hands on the railing, palms down. His cloak was black and covered with holographic green digits that seemed to give it a sheen from a distance. Up close, it was as if some great cosmic instruction code were inscribed on cloth.

"Did you think about pitching your tools overboard?" He said after a moment.

Cray smirked, but shifted back a step. "Guess I'm not the first one?"

"No. Hardly. I once stood in your sandals myself. Only I let go of a screwdriver."

There was a pause as the elder looked over the edge. Cray could sense a bit of warped nostalgia here but said nothing.

Stanwick continued. "Know what happened? Nothing. Oh sure. There were a few sparks. Yet the thing bounced off one of the rollers down there and shot across the room. No harm done. No, Jupiter didn't swing out of alignment, nor did the moons of Saturn fly out of their orbits."

Cray relaxed his shoulders.

"Then I spent the next week having to take apart and clean several of the machines. Messy work."

Cray turned back towards the gearbox in front of him. "Say, I was trying to push this last gear into place. Could I get a hand?"

The elder strode over to the gear, which was a foot across and lying on the grated floor. He picked it up with ease and pushed it into place in the assembly overhead.

"How did you do that? I struggled for an hour on that." Cray circled around and stared up at the assembly while Stanwick reached up and threw the run switch. The array of gears, belts, and pulleys churned to life.

Stanwick then picked up the bronze-colored panel which leaned next to the railing and clicked it into place. He looked down at the toolset on the floor and then over to Cray. "This isn't a car or a factory back on Earth. It's not a grandfather clock in your grandma's living room either. Pick up your tools and follow me." Stanwick then flipped up his hood and walked away.

"But I have more…"

The elder stopped, hands clasped, and stood waiting.

Cray reached down and picked up his toolset bag along with a chronowrench that sat close to the edge of the catwalk floor. Part of him still wanted to kick it overboard just to watch the sparks fly.

"Please don't do that." Stanwick said.

Cray picked up the chronowrench and stuffed it into his tool bag. *This elder was good.* Too good at reading his actions, even with his back turned.

Cray followed the elder along the catwalks back to the maintenance elevator and back down to the transit floor. From there they walked through a narrow hallway and out into a skyway. The skyway arched over a shimmering emerald and pale blue stream that looked unlike any water he had seen on Earth.

After the bridge, they entered a building with pristine, white-and-green trimmed hallways. In minutes they arrived in silence to a vast room full of computers and whirring machines.

The elder motioned towards a desk off to the left. "Set your tools there."

Cray set his tools aside and folded his hands like the elder. He still did not put his hood up. The last thing he felt like was a spiritual and vow-abiding monk. As the day dragged on he felt more like a hack automobile mechanic back in the garage where his father first taught him how to fix and repair cars. Like his Dad's garage he was one bad oil change away from losing the opportunity altogether.

Stanwick then walked into the center of the room and motioned to Cray. "Here. Let me show you something."

Cray walked over but unclasped his hands. Five and a half more months of this was now beginning to look to him like a long term trip to prison.

"When you finish your work in the mechanical center, you'll be trained here. But only after your six month postulant time is up. At that point you must make a choice whether to press on and take your vows or return back to Earth."

Cray let his shoulders sag and he took a deep breath. "Six months of being a grease monkey inside a giant factory? I've done worse, but I was hoping for more."

"It's not a factory. Those presses you maintain are the last stage of a most amazing process. But only those with faith advance and truly see it for what it is."

Cray rolled his eyes and looked around the vast room of machines before him. There were no gears here, just row after row of terminals as far as the eye could see and monks in black and green cloaks fixated on their screens. The lighting was dimmer here than on the printing press floor but the screens seemed to illuminate the green digits on their cloaks. Cray's cloak, however, seemed to blend in with the wooden floor beneath him. "Faith. Is that your answer to everything?" He mumbled.

"No, but it is a skill you'll have to master, let alone wield."

"Look. Maybe I'm not your guy. I know I chose to come here for my community service time, but it's like everywhere I turn I get stuck. Besides, what does faith have to do with how I use a chronowrench? What's it have to do with code?"

At the sound of his raised voice, several of the monks stopped typing at the green-screened terminals before them. A half-dozen turned their heads towards Cray. Only when Cray looked away did they turn back to their keyboards. The room was soon filled with clacking keys again.

"Faith drives this entire system," Stanwick said. "Where the mechanical ends, faith begins. Faith is the bridge from the tactile to the impossible. It's up to you to cross over it."

Stanwick turned away from him as if to survey the room. He abruptly turned back and urged Cray to follow again. "As you know, you are free to leave any time you wish. I'm sure there are plenty of ditches back on Earth that need the garbage picked up out of them."

"Look, hey, I have to be honest with you. I made a deal with the judge back home. If I stayed here six months, I'd be free afterwards."

Stanwick smiled weakly. "I know. You're not the first and you won't be the last."

* * *

At the end of the six month probation period, Cray sat up at the edge of his bed in his apartment and watched out the window as a pair of birds he did not recognize alighted onto a nearby tree branch and then flew off. In two hours he would be asked an important question as he stood at the crossroads of his future: whether he should ship off back to home or commit to a set of vows he had become increasingly fond of over the past month.

He stood up and paced over to the kitchenette where he opened the refrigerator and perused its contents. Cold pizza, milk, a half head of lettuce (which was expensive in these parts of the galaxy), and some strange-looking, blue, star-shaped fruit another postulant recommended. None of it looked interesting since he slept poorly last night and his stomach was not in want of anything. He flipped on the coffee maker on the counter and made a fresh pot of coffee.

He ran his hands through his hair, then took a shower, and followed it up with a cup of bitter coffee. From the coat rack near the door he picked up his cloak, tied the beige rope tight around the middle, and slipped on his sandals. He remembered now how he had dreamt last night of code. More specifically, of coding at a terminal and wearing a green digit covered cloak and taking his place amongst the many concentric desks in the systems center.

After a short walk, he looked up at the monastery building one last time before entering. It was a sprawling complex of glass and steel, built like three concentric rings. From the air it probably looked like a spider web with sparkling streams between each ring and bridges arching over the streams to join the rings together. All along the outer ring of the monastery were towers every two hundred feet which reminded him of a castle back on Earth.

As he entered the monastery, he gazed on at the inscription arching over the front doors: "Mechanics. Coders. Scribes. Building Bridges by Faith." The cryptic inscription was gibberish to him six months ago but he realized that beyond the computer system center he had seen in the second ring several months ago was the true heart of the operation. The mysterious ring three was seldom discussed amongst novices, frequently discussed amongst postulants, and dwelled on continually by himself.

Inside, it took several minutes for his eyes to adjust. Once he had passed down the long, darkened entry hallway, he came into the sentry way for the computer center. The camera system at the entry scanned his figure and as he watched the green fuzzy beam rove down his cloak, he wondered all the while about his future and where he would be an hour from now. Many postulants had speculated about the nature of the entry interviews and none of the outgoing monks or new novices spoke a word of their meetings.

Stanwick met him in the sentry way and they both walked into another secluded room with no windows, a table, and two wooden chairs. The elder peeled back his hood, revealing a graying beard, a scramble of short gray hair on top of his head, and a faded black and gray mustache. He sat down in one chair while Cray sat opposite him on the other side of the table.

"Shall we begin?" Stanwick said, not using any type of notebook or writing device to take notes. He smiled briefly.

Cray sat upright in his chair and folded his hands before him.

"When you dropped the bolt into the press, what happened?"

The question was like a punch in the gut. Maybe even the kidneys. Cray did not think anybody saw him do it, especially since it occurred last week when he was entirely on his own. He closed his eyes a moment and took a deep breath. "It hit a gear, ricocheted off another, and shot across the room."

"Did the world fall off its axis? Did the sun stop rising? Did the planets fly out of alignment?"

"No. I mean, I...don't know. They're only printing presses, right?

I've seen the books they print. I can't understand a word of 'em."

"Good."

Cray swallowed hard.

"When you snuck a glimpse into the ring three, what did you see?"

Another gut punch.

"I saw a library. A few computer terminals. Oh, and white cloaks. And books. Books with fire for letters. It was like they were writing with pens that were dripping with fire."

"Good." Stanwick leaned back in his chair and crossed his arms. "Do you know how long it takes to be a novice?"

"Six months, maybe more."

The elder withdrew a book from his cloak and set it on the table before Cray. "Do you know what this is?"

Cray reached out and picked up the book. The cover, table of contents, and beyond looked to be written in a language completely unlike anything he had ever seen on Earth. "I...I don't know what this is. Looks kind of like what came off the factory press the other week."

"It's the Word. Do you know what we do in the inner monastery? Or ring three as some people call it?"

Cray closed the book and slid it back towards the elder. "I haven't a clue."

"We translate the Word for other planets. Far and wide. Until the whole universe hears."

In that moment the inscription over the doorway made sense to Cray. He looked up from the table and then at Stanwick.

Stanwick then picked up the book and slid it back into his cloak. "Have you decided? You're free to go of course. Since you've served your community service time according to the judge back on Earth."

Cray leaned back in his chair. "I need to know the answer to one question. Has anybody ever tried to break the computer systems?"

"Many have. All have failed."

"What do they do with the ones who've tried?"

"They make them scribes."

"If I..."

"Yes."

The two sat in silence, neither one showing expression. Cray then folded his hands together and leaned forward. "When do I start?"

The elder grinned. "Today. Right now in fact. Once you take your vows, of course."

"Then what?"

"Then you learn how to code. I do think you'll make a fine coder."

Stanwick stood up and opened a panel in the wall. He withdrew a black and green digit covered cloak and held it out to Cray. "And you'll make an even better scribe."

Between the Lines

She was a work of art with attitude and a sight to behold from a distance. Up close, Dmitri found her way with words mesmerizing and her conversations captivating. He sat face to face with her now, and while she worked, he reminisced about the night they first met.

He found her on a rainy night while digging through some files on his late father's computer. It was an accident, really, but once his eyes locked in on her he knew his life would never return to normal again. Dmitri learned quickly of her grace, beauty, and abilities. Together they would play a fiction game where he would give her bits of information, ideas, and character sketches and she would weave them into works of literary art.

"SANDRA, old girl, you've done it again," he said to her and then punched the enter button on the keyboard. She replied in kind by sending the novel to the printer on the desk next to him. He pulled the pages off of the printer and read through the first chapter one last time. To him, it sounded as if it were written by a human author.

He then printed off the rest of the book and bound each half together with a large, black, plastic clip. At over two hundred and fifty pages, the only thing he could see in it was cash. Easy cash to be exact. He stuffed the manuscript into a manila envelope and raced to his car.

An hour later he pulled up to a small, black and gray commercial building on the edge of downtown Cincinnati. He clutched the manuscript tight under his arm and entered the building. With a broad smile he bounded up the carpeted staircase leading to the second floor and found the agent's office. He stopped to check his hair in the glass pane of the office door and stepped inside.

The reception area was a study in oak, brass, and frosted glass but Dmitri was more interested in studying the receptionist instead. She sat in a black swivel chair with her back half-turned towards him, filing her fire-engine red nails and cradling a phone on her shoulder.

After she hung up the phone and before she could turn completely towards him, he spoke up. "I'm here to see Mr. Jenkins."

"I'll let him know you're here." She picked up the phone again and buzzed the agent.

Dmitri tapped the top of the desk impatiently with his free hand. He leaned over. Bored already, he studied her hands and her fiery red, curly hair.

"Mr. Chekov," said a quiet, raspy voice from behind him.

Dmitri spun around and stuck out a hand to shake.

"Sorry for your loss. Your dad was one of the best authors we've ever seen. His technique was incredible. And I never heard a bad word about his kids."

Dmitri gave him the biggest smile he could muster, but frankly, he was glad the old man was out of the picture. He handed Jenkins the envelope as if to cut off any further conversation on the subject.

Jenkins motioned towards the left. "Can we take a look at this in my office?"

Dmitri nodded without another word and followed him to the office. The two men sat down into black leather chairs opposite each other. Dmitri leaned forward and interlocked his fingers, spinning his thumbs around until Jenkins stared at him.

Jenkins set the folder on his desk and slid the manuscript out. He read the title aloud. "The Perils of September. Hmmm. Interesting. What genre is it again?"

Dmitri stared at Jenkins, all the while fighting the urge to roll his eyes. *Was this guy for real?*

"It's science fiction," Dmitri said after a few seconds.

Jenkins read the first page, then the next, and leafed through some others. "Not his...uh...strongest material. Where'd you say you found this?"

"I found a copy of the first part on the hard drive of his computer. I saw the other part in paper form in a box in his attic." Dmitri stared at the shelves behind Jenkins. It was a study in clutter, with naval awards, photos of time spent in the service, and a dusty eagle statue of some sort on another shelf. There were two photos of grandchildren, a painted plastic model submarine, and several small orange pumpkins like the kind you find in cardboard bins at the grocery store in the fall.

Jenkins continued to read and flipped another page. Then he leaned back in his chair and put his hands behind his neck. He was a thin rail of a man with patches of gray hair above his ears and had a thin, wiry mustache. After a moment of staring towards the window he stared back at Dmitri.

"Something wrong?" Dmitri said in an attempt to study the agent.

"You're not trying to blow one past me are you?"

"What do you mean?" Dmitri leaned back in his chair, tapping his foot.

"Oh, I don't know. I mean, I've read tons of your father's books over the years. Rough drafts, short stories, half starts to novels, that sort of thing. This feels…what's the word I'm looking for…it feels like a hodgepodge of ideas."

Dmitri felt his cheeks become flush. "But I found that on his computer. It's his. Maybe he didn't want to show it to you. It's good. Keep reading. Trust me."

"I'll read it. As a favor. How do I put this…your Dad's genius was the ability to take several great ideas and distill them into one or two great ones." Jenkins picked up the manuscript again and stared at one of the pages for a few seconds. "This feels like ideas from other writers sort of slammed together."

"So what are you saying? It's not sellable?"

"I don't know. I'll have to finish it. It's kind of a muddy start. Disjointed, even. Did he run this by Sandra?"

"Sandra?"

"Your dad never told you about Sandy? Some secret writing partner of his. I guess she would read his manuscripts and offer suggestions. He started using her in his later years before sending things to us."

Dmitri pretended to sit and think about this a moment. "Come to think of it, he's mentioned Sandra before. I don't know if he ran this by her or not."

"Hmmm. The dialogue here on page four is cold. Almost soulless."

Dmitri sprang up from his chair and strode over to the agent's desk. He lunged for the manuscript. "Here. I'll take it. I'll find someone else who knows talent when they see it."

Jenkins moved his hand over the manuscript. "Easy, easy. I'll read it to the end. It's probably just a throwaway beginning. Look, I'll give you a call when I finish it. I wasn't trying to insult your dad or his legacy or anything like that. Honest."

Dmitri backed away and gave the agent a thin smile. He extended a hand to shake. "I'm looking forward to working with you."

* * *

A couple of weeks later Dmitri sat in his computer desk chair again. He watched SANDRA weave her wit into a new tale, this time working over an incomplete novel he found on the computer hard drive the night before. He had not lied to Jenkins about the origin of the first manuscript, but when he originally found the book on his father's hard drive it was only thirty pages long. At best, the original story was a pile of half-thought-out ideas and incomplete character sketches.

To plug the gaps, he let SANDRA pull ideas from other famous works, including his father's own successful novels, in an act of veiled plagiarism. The old man's worst day at the computer, after all, was surely gold now for all his adoring fans.

Dmitri looked over at a newspaper that sat next to the computer monitor. He read of yet another story about his father, that used words like "posthumous" and "master" and "work of genius" in a single paragraph alone. In disgust he pushed the paper off the desk and into the wastebasket below.

A minute later, SANDRA finished and began to print out a paper copy. As the pages came off the printer, he scribbled in dozens of vague comments in the margins. He admired his Da Vinci handiwork until the phone rang.

"Dmitri. Hi, it's Jenkins. Say, I looked over the manuscript. My original feelings still stand. Have anything else for us?"

"I just happen to be holding a real masterpiece in my hands as we speak. I'll send it right over."

* * *

A month passed without a word from the agent. Dmitri found yet another piece of the novel on the computer and was sure the next installment would land him the book deal of a lifetime. He had already sent the first installment of a detective novel to Jenkins and told him he had to rummage around to find the second part.

The phone rang one afternoon. It was Jenkins, and this time Dmitri knew he had hit a home run.

"This one's better. A lot better. Still not where I'd like it to be, but with some work I think it's sellable."

Dmitri pumped his fist and leaned back in his desk chair. He had not fully read this last manuscript, but he knew it was a crime or detective novel of some sort. He reached over to tap the top of the computer monitor as if he were patting a dog on the head.

"Did you see what he wrote on page 83? About the new clues at the crime scene? Brilliant."

"What can I tell you. The guy was a genius."

"You said there's a second part, right?"

"That's right. I have it right here."

"Great. I can't wait to see what he does with that storyline about the computer."

"What do you mean?"

"About the evidence on the computer. I'm betting it's the guy's brother or maybe his old business partner that did it. But there's something mysterious about his computer."

Dmitri cringed and tried to look over the paper manuscript in his hands in a hurry. After a page or two of skimming he gave up. His Dad always did have a vivid imagination but some days the prose just bored him to sleep.

"You still there?" Jenkins' less than enthusiastic voice crackled after a minute of silence.

"I'm still here. Look, I'll send over the rest of the book. Overnight mail if you want."

"Fantastic. I think we got a winner here."

* * *

Another month went by before Dmitri was called back into Jenkins' office. Dmitri showed up early for his appointment after spending the entire car ride over to the office fantasizing about days on the beach and nights at the casino.

Dmitri shook Jenkins' hand upon entering the room and sat down across from him. By the beaming expression on the agent's face, he knew his fortunes were about to change.

"Great work finding this. Still a bit choppy and disjointed in places, but it's workable. Let me ask you something," Jenkins said.

"Shoot."

"Were you and your dad close near the end?"

Dmitri pressed his back into the chair and wondered where this conversation was going. "Sometimes. Some days were better than others. Why?"

"Okay. Look, the storyline is good, but it caught me by surprise. Towards the end it gets sort of autobiographical with witnesses in the story describing the main character's last days."

Dmitri remained unmoved.

"The thing is, a lot of it paralleled your dad's own last days, especially the hospital parts. I wonder if Sandra said anything to you about him."

Dmitri could feel his heart rate accelerate and his face becoming flush again. He drummed his fingers on the armrest and tapped his foot to a similar tempo.

The agent paused a moment and gave him a confused look. "Didn't you read what he wrote?"

"Some of it."

"Here's the part that got me. I read the ending over and over but he never answered the whole question of the book: who killed the main character? That guy was loved by the community, donated money to great causes, and had a decent reputation. Yet you go through the story and some major suspects are eliminated. By the end, there's only two left. It's either his kid or his old business partner. And the computer. What's up with the computer? He claims on page 164 it's a treasure trove of evidence."

Dmitri sank lower in his chair. By now he started to fantasize about the fastest way out of the room.

Jenkins cleared his throat. "You alright?"

"I'm...I'm fine."

"You're white as a ghost. Anyway, where was I...oh yes, the computer. I don't know what to think. By the way, are you good at writing? Did the old man ever show you any tricks of the trade?"

"I tried writing a couple of stories once. When I was a teenager."

Jenkins leaned back in his chair and swiveled back and forth. "Okay. Look, we can work that out later. Maybe we should talk about the potential advances on this."

Dmitri laughed a bit to ease the tension in the room. "Bills are getting tight. I can only turn the heat down so far in my house."

"Right. Hey, I just thought of something. Your dad used to play this little game with his manuscripts."

"What kind of game?"

"He used to bury extra things about his stories or the characters in weird places in the text. One day he let me in on his system." Jenkins reached into his desk and pulled out a sheet of paper with some writing on it. He held it up for Dmitri to see.

"See this? It's a decoder. Your dad always had this weird fascination with cryptography. He'd use certain obscure words in his manuscripts and when they'd appear on this key, the word would represent a letter. Sometimes he'd use this device to answer a question that was posed in another part of the story." Jenkins laughed. "This key is so weird. Who uses words like dodecahedron in their fiction anyway?"

Dmitri's eyes began to burn. There was nothing on his father's computer about keys, cryptography, or buried codes. *What next?*

Jenkins chuckled and pulled out a piece of blank paper. He called Dmitri over to his side. "Look. I remember this word back on page 29."

Jenkins pulled out a pen and matched the word with the appropriate letter on the key. "Maybe it's a clue as to whom the guilty suspect is."

Dmitri watched in horror as Jenkins wrote down the letter "d" on the blank page. He watched Jenkins flip through several more chapters until he found another match. Next came the letter "m", followed by the letter "i".

"That's weird. There's no one in the story by that name."

Dmitri backed away from the desk and edged towards the door.

"T," Jenkins said. He looked up.

Dmitri dove for the door handle.

As Jenkins dropped his pen and reached for the phone, Dmitri bolted out the door and down the hallway. He flew down the stairs, not once looking back, with his feet barely touching the steps.

Corridors

The Great Zoltini reclined in his chair and stared out into the blackness of space, then back down at the just-as-empty blank screen in front of him. He picked up his fifteen-stringed, triple-necked ionitar and strummed out a chord from his last hit song that not been heard on the interstellar radio bands for twenty years now.

In front of him sat Mark, his longtime pilot, and Melinda, the longtime navigational and systems analyst. Mark slowed the ion drive engines and toggled the heads-up display on the console before him. A cool, indigo glow filled the cockpit.

"This view never gets old," Mark said.

"Say did you see that comet smack Neptune?" Melinda replied.

"No. When was that?"

"Just a minute ago according to the long range scope."

The Great Zoltini tried to eye the display for himself. "Where are we by the way?"

Mark turned to glance back. "Passing by the Sol system."

"Sol. Never heard of it. Any music halls down there...on what did you say? Neptune?"

"No. There should be some on Earth."

"Earth? Never heard of it. It's inhabited, right? Surely they never heard of the Great Zoltini there." Zoltini raised up his right hand and gestured towards the window as if looking out upon a vast crowd. "Famed in seven star systems and soon to be eight!"

"I hate to burst your bubble, but it looks like a funny system," Melinda said.

"If they have cities and music halls, let's go." Zoltini stood up and held both hands up in the air. "Imagine the roar of the crowd. Thousands upon thousands of new fans. The Great Zoltini will rise again!"

"I wouldn't get my hopes up. Something's wrong here. Look at the scope."

Melinda pointed to a high-definition scanner display in front of her. Mark and Zoltini leaned over to observe.

"Scanner here says Earth has a visitor. And it isn't us," Melinda said.

Mark flipped through star system charts on his monitor and then ran a cross-system check with the onboard celestial database. No results came back. "What does the visitor look like?"

"It's a cubic ship. That can't be right."

More levers were lifted, more databases dialed up, and more scanners were started.

"It's not big enough to exert a pull on us, at least not yet." Melinda said after a moment. "Scanner says it's about twelve to thirteen hundred miles across."

Mark leaned back in his chair and rested his chin on his folded hands. "It's a ship. A big ship. If it's headed for Earth where's it going to land?"

"We don't have enough fuel to investigate up close. If we make an arc and get within a few million miles we can always run the lower range scanners on it."

Melinda typed in the new flight path into the onboard navigation computer. Suddenly, a female voice from the navigation system said, "This is not an established travel corridor. Risks of accidents are likely. Continue?"

Mark and Melinda looked back at Zoltini. Zoltini motioned towards the window. "Yes! Continue!"

"Hey, look at this," Melinda said, pointing towards her monitor. "We might get a detailed view of this thing in about an hour or so."

Zoltini stared on at the computer as a visual image of the object finally came into view. The object appeared to be a substantial cube, and at certain moments its surface reflected the dim, distant sunlight, throwing off a rainbow of colors as if it were composed of thousands of tiny prisms. "I wonder if it is using the interstellar bands. Melinda, see what you can find."

"I'm getting a funny reading on the scanner. The ship, or whatever it is, is covered with some type of lettering. Don't recognize the language, though," Mark said.

"Still on target for Earth, too? Where's it going to land? I thought

Earth was full of water and land masses," Melinda replied.

"Better check your history. According to the databank, the water was scorched off a year ago or so."

"The sun doesn't look abnormal. No supernova. Must have been a flare."

"That's one big flare. Run the scanner data against the database."

"I did. No known matches against any ships in this sector."

Mark and Melinda tapped away at their keyboards as the sun in the fore window grew to the size of a pea.

"You say the planet's been scorched, though?" Zoltini said with a tinge of defeat in his voice.

"Refined like it was in a smelter's furnace," Mark said.

"Any tractor beams?" Melinda asked.

"None."

"Weapons?"

"None."

"Signs of life?"

"Definitely. It's like a squared planet if that were even possible."

"Colonization?"

"Good point. But you said the databanks have no match for it. Unless it came from another dimension."

Melinda leaned back in her chair. "But it looks like a giant city. According to an ancient Earth book in the database it comes through the clouds and lands."

"But there is no more Earth. No water, no land, no people, no books…"

"Maybe they fled to the city spaceship. Or whatever it is. It looks like it has a name."

There was silence in the cockpit for a good half minute.

"It looks like it goes by the name of New Jerusalem," Melinda said.

Zoltini moved back towards the computer consoles. On the screen before him was a faint image of clouds enveloping a brown disc. "What's that?"

"Earth," Melinda said.

"Where are the cities? But you say the ship is a city?"

"Yes. I'm starting to get something on the interstellar bands."

"Put it on! Let's hear it," Zoltini gestured.

Melinda twisted a couple of knobs and clicked a few keys on her keyboard.

Zoltini paced about the room excitedly. "Perhaps this city ship has great music halls in it."

Suddenly the cockpit was filled with music and voices singing. It sounded like choirs upon choirs singing with harmonies Zoltini doubted he could replicate. He returned to his chair and slumped back down in silence. He gazed down at his triple-necked ionitar and then back at Mark. "Can you record this? Get this! Hurry!"

Zoltini picked up his instrument but did not know where to begin. He put his fingers on a fretboard and wanted to strike a chord but his hands began to tremble instead. For minutes he sat in humble silence.

He set the instrument down and typed a handful of notes onto his machine. "Such music," he said. "I have never heard such sounds. Are you recording this?"

"Yes," said Mark.

"I…I can't play here. At this city. Is there any place to land?"

"It doesn't look like it."

Zoltini felt such a surge of depression well up within him that he did not think he had the strength to stand, much less play a note. The music was so unlike anything he had ever heard anywhere else and part of him was in awe. It saddened him to think he could never write music such as this, but then a thought came to him.

"Still want to try and visit Earth?" Melinda said.

"No. Keep recording. Tell no one of this inspiration." Zoltini stood up from his chair and felt a joy rushing back into his features. He gestured wildly towards the window. "The Great Zoltini will rise again. Famed in seven star systems and soon to unveil his latest masterpiece!"

In Remembrance of Simplicity

Dr. Hanwick,

Since I last wrote to you, my research has taken an exciting turn. After several weeks of experiments involving the tapping of my nervous system circuits via neurological electrodes and after months of exhaustive preparation and research, I feel I am ready to undergo my most daring experiment to date.

Plans are in place for the implantation of a high capacity, low-power memory chip into my cerebral cortex. The procedure itself should only take an hour or two, but if my research is accurate, the end result should be an expanded, durable memory system that is not prone to tiredness, age, alcohol, or stress. As we all know, the memory system Mother Nature gave us is good, but could use some improvement.

I'm being implanted with a one terabyte chip, which should be sufficient for basic testing purposes. This is not a blank chip, however, since it contains a ROM component. It also comes complete with a dictionary and an almanac fact book from the past year. Can you imagine me on Jeopardy?

All the best,
Dr. Alcomb

Dr. Hanwick,

Good news. The memory chip implantation procedure I elaborated upon in our previous correspondence was an unparalleled success. Other than some minor irritation on my scalp, the electrodes, the circuitry, and my system's response to it all appears wonderfully stable.

I've tested the dictionary database in its totality and have found eloquent new words to exercise in conversations with my colleagues. When asked to elaborate on their definitions, I am able to instantly recall the full definition as well as offering synonyms, antonyms, and alternate spellings. I've also been able to access a vast array of new facts but am afraid I've become a bore in conversations as I readily have newfound cognitive abilities surpassing most others in the room.

I've also noticed that I've found trivia shows on television to be just that…trivial. I seriously wonder how some of these participants are selected as their knowledge is woefully lacking and deficient in multiple areas. They are ill-suited for the task at hand.

An oddity: today I witnessed the scene of a rear-end car collision between a white Lexus and a teal pickup truck. It is difficult to elaborate, but I felt as though I could see the accident coming seconds ahead of time. Before, during, and after the crash my mind continually captured and stored images, much like a high-speed camera snapping photographs for minutes on end.

I was then able to later recall all visual and aural aspects of the accident with effortless ease. In fact, that night my dreams were filled with images from the incident.

There are some days when it seems like I cannot walk into a room without absorbing every available visual detail. I'm recording all of this in my journal entries.

All the best,
Dr. Alcomb

Dr. Hanwick,

It has been a strange, alienating week. I am now experiencing almost nightmarish recall of even the most mundane details of life. Useless information. What did I eat for lunch last Tuesday? Salisbury steak, mashed potatoes, and green beans with a high sodium content. I ate this meal at 12:07 in the afternoon in the cafeteria which was forty-three percent full. I can tell you precisely who sat where and when, what they ate, what clothing they wore, who they sat with, and even the newspapers they were reading. I can tell you which ones seemed to like their food and which ones seem preoccupied. I can tell you these details and much more for every day this week. Did you know the third fluorescent light fixture from the window is in need of replacement?

Last night I stayed up most of the night and flipped through several volumes of an old encyclopedia set from years ago. Did you know there is a disease called synesthesia? It's a neurological condition where stimulation of one sense automatically activates a secondary response in a different sense. For instance, when a person looks at the number three in a book, they perceive it as being colored red even if the original color is black. In other cases, a person may hear a sound, such as a train horn, and end up smelling an unrelated odor such as a rose bush.

I noticed colleagues are avoiding me. My own wife sleeps on the couch now. I eat lunch alone, I work alone. Learning is now becoming a chore. I'm more interested in seeing how fast I can learn rather than what I can learn.

The headaches are increasing. At night my dreams are becoming increasingly disjointed, as if my brain is trying to process billions of bits of information but somehow can't.

In two days I will have the implant removed.

All the best,
Dr. Alcomb

Michael Galloway

Dr. Hanwick,

I almost did not write this letter to you until I saw a reply from you in the mail. I had to go back over my journal notes to see why I was even writing to you. My notes were like the words of a stranger.

Regarding the operation, the removal was a success. There was one complication.

My notes talk of witnessing a car accident in vivid detail a few weeks ago. I don't remember it. Yet today in the mail I received a letter from a legal firm requesting that they meet with me to discuss details of the accident. Perhaps the chip will be seized by the authorities as evidence.

My notes also referred to my experiences watching trivia shows on television. I watched one yesterday and did not get a single question right. My wife called me a "walking dictionary" last night but all I could do was stutter.

This morning when I awoke she served me breakfast in bed. I asked her why she made me a waffle covered in strawberries with bacon on the side and she said they were my favorite things to eat for breakfast.

As I write this now, I've let my food go cold. Outside of my window there is a large green and blue dragonfly sitting on one of my wife's red and yellow sunflowers. I wonder when it will fly away.

All the best,
Dr. Alcomb

The Mines of Mars, Part I

Transport Seven would be coming along soon now, Kyrk thought, and would make a stop at the Tranquility Outpost, but of course, no one would be home. In the confusion he would seize the transport, plunder its contents, and leave without a trace.

Or so that was the plan he dreamt up in his head earlier that week. He watched through his binoculars as the silver-white transport train emerged from between a series of cinnamon-colored hills and slid towards the station, gliding above the Martian sands on a dual set of rails.

He turned and handed his binoculars to Goldman, who stood next to him. At just over five feet tall, Goldman had a bulked-up build but no sense of spatial reasoning. Kyrk met Goldman months ago working a similar job.

"How far is it down to the platform?" Goldman asked, as he fiddled with the focus knob.

"It's a three hundred foot run downhill on rock. Then another three hundred feet across the open desert. Assuming the station workers don't pick up on our presence, we'll then have about two minutes to clear out the post and then it's show time."

"But I thought you said there were a hundred cars in this train. I ain't ever hit one like this."

Kyrk gave him a broad smile. "Me either."

Goldman then handed back the binoculars. He pointed to the two large, black, cloth sacks lying on the ground next to them. "How much bullion did you say we could carry in these sacks?"

"We're not going to carry them. We'll load them up and then drop them to the sands below. Then we'll bury the bags and come back for them later on."

Kyrk motioned towards the desert valley below. "Let's head out. The train should hit the station in a few minutes."

They scrambled down the rocky incline towards the valley floor, and slipped through a rocky crevice full of jagged edges until they made it to the bottom. As their boots hit the sand it kicked up a cloud of fine red dust that hung in the air like puffs of smoke. The blue glow of dawn threw just enough light onto the sand so that they were able to move with stealth-like grace towards the outpost.

Kyrk made it to the base of the train platform in a matter of minutes. He heard Goldman right behind him and paused a moment at one of the giant, steel, cylindrical columns that supported the station.

There were eight columns in all and on opposite ends of the platform were maintenance ladders that ran down to the ground. He figured scaling a ladder would be the easy part. Timing the strike on the occupants inside would be where all the risks occurred.

Kyrk scaled one of the ladders and Goldman followed close behind. As Kyrk's boots hit each rung, he could see tiny clouds of desert dust radiate out as if his legs were pistons on a steam locomotive. To him, it looked as if the ladders had never been used and soon he wondered whether this was one of those unoccupied stations.

Kyrk stopped short of the top of the ladder and pulled out a hand mirror. He cocked it to scan the building for signs of life but only saw a dashboard of green and red indicator lamps. Curious, he stuck his head up just high enough to peer into the station. The building was dark, save for the outdoor illumination lamps near the station sign and along the edge of the track where it met the platform. He waved back down at Goldman and nodded his head towards the platform.

In a rush, he bounded up the rest of the rungs and pounced onto the platform in expectation. When nothing happened, he punched in the airlock code on the silver panel to his right. The door slid open and revealed an empty station full of blue-tinged shadows.

Goldman arrived next and together they explored the outpost. It reminded Kyrk of an old abandoned bus depot he saw back on Earth as a kid, but here they were no crinkled-up newspapers, graffiti, or smells of urine.

The place had an untouched feel to it as if it were constructed by humans one season and then abandoned to automation thereafter. Kyrk peered over the control panel which looked more like a monitor with only a handful of knobs and buttons for emergency manual control. He did not see any cameras anywhere inside the station and began to wonder what purpose it even served. Outside the window he could see a platform, some one hundred feet in length and another hundred feet in depth as if it were a passenger railroad depot back on Earth.

"What do you make of this place?" Goldman said, as he stared out the window.

"It makes for one lonely passenger station. What I don't get is why it's unoccupied. No robots, no cameras, no people."

"Maybe the map we looked at was wrong."

"Wrong as in out of date or wrong as in deliberately wrong? That's the question."

"Think it's a trap?"

"We'll find out in a minute. Look down the track."

Kyrk pointed down the rail line which faded off into the hills. Further down the track a tiny beam of white light lit up the rails. Transport Seven was right on time. He turned to Goldman. "Got your pistol ready?"

"I thought we weren't going to kill anyone."

"Stun, not kill. I'm getting a bad feeling about this one, kid. We'll hang out in here like we rehearsed and then swing around on the ledge in front of the building."

Kyrk watched and waited as the narrow beam of light on the train engine pierced the faint light of dawn and grew in diameter. The transport trains had been known to travel at nearly 150 miles per hour and this one looked to be going only about fifty, as if it were weighted down. He had expected to see fifty or more mining cars in tow since that is what the manifest stated, but instead there were only twenty or so ore cars on the train and thirty boxcars.

"I thought you said this was an ore train," Goldman said.

"Some of it is. The boxcars are what we want. That's where the silver and indium bullion is. The keys are cars twenty-five and twenty-six."

They both crouched down behind the control panel as the light from the engine illuminated the platform and then the interior of the building. Kyrk watched as the transport glided to a halt next to the station. He paused a moment, anticipating the engineer to climb down from the engine cab.

Several minutes passed before a figure dressed in a dark blue spacesuit and helmet scaled down the ladder on the lead engine. The man appeared to stop in mid-step on the ladder as if he picked up on something being wrong about the situation.

Kyrk held his breath while the figure pounced onto the platform and approached the station. "In five...four...three..."

Kyrk and Goldman exploded out of the door and rounded the front of the station, pistols drawn on the figure. By the time the man in the dark blue suit was only a few feet from the engine, Kyrk was standing five feet in front of him.

"Hi. Nice morning for a drive isn't it?" Kyrk said, pointing his pistol at the engineer's chest.

"Please don't shoot. Take what you want."

"What's in the boxcars?"

"Food."

"Food? Your manifest said this is an ore train. What's in twenty-five and twenty-six back there? It's not ore and it's not food."

Before the man could finish Kyrk fired off a stun shot from his gun and dropped the engineer to the platform like a deflated balloon.

"Let's search the cab. Make sure he's alone," Kyrk said after stepping around the dark blue heap before him.

Goldman climbed the engine ladder and slipped inside the cab. Thirty seconds later he emerged and gave Kyrk a thumbs-up signal. "How do you intend on checking cars twenty-five and twenty-six?" He asked after landing back onto the platform.

Kyrk tucked his pistol back into a pocket and zipped it shut. "We do it the old-fashioned way. We walk across the tops of the cars."

"I...I'm not good with heights."

"Only one way to overcome that."

Kyrk climbed up onto the first boxcar behind the engine and began to walk across the top of it. By now, the full light of the Martian dawn began to overtake the sky, softly illuminating the train and rails with a reddish-gold glow. The train threw long shadows onto the sands below, which suddenly looked further down than he first thought.

He heard Goldman's boots ascend the steel boxcar rungs behind him. He then jumped over the gap between the first and second boxcars and felt his footing become surer with every step. Soon, he ran across the tops of the cars.

By car fifteen, the lighting improved and he knew he would only have a limited amount of time to secure the cargo and pitch it overboard onto the rust-colored sands below. He turned back to see Goldman plodding along across the top of car number eight. A part of him began to regret his choice of a travelling companion.

Kyrk accelerated until he came upon car twenty-five. He slowed to a crawl at the end of car twenty-four and crouched down. He turned to see Goldman still several cars behind and still poking along. He wondered at what point the engineer would wake up and climb back into the engine. When that happened he knew he would dread the long trip down to the sands below. A scraping noise from below made him freeze at the top of the ladder.

He extended the microphone attached to his spacesuit and put its cupped sensor against the roof of the boxcar and listened. Other than the faint approaching footsteps of Goldman, he heard what sounded like a crying infant. Then came what sounded like the faint echoes of a soothing mother's voice, followed by a man's voice shouting at the mother and child.

He scrambled down the side ladder, boots clomping out against the metal rungs until he was able to jump onto the bridge below. The space between the bridge's guardrail and the boxcar was barely big enough to squeeze through. When he came to the sliding doors of the car, he pressed the microphone sensor against the wall again.

This time there was silence. Then came the restless shifting on the floor of the car as if several people were inside. Kyrk flipped open the bars on the door and slid one of them open with all his might.

He shone a flashlight inside and several sets of eyes and dirtied faces inside of space suits stared back at him. As his flashlight swept across the interior, he counted fifty or more people inside of all ages and races.

"Here I thought it was a car full of bullion," he said in disappointment. He turned away and dowsed his light and looked down the tracks at car twenty-six. His shoulders slumped. Was the whole train like this?

In the distance he saw the dust clouds from Goldman's boots across the metal roofs of the cars further up the line. He turned his back on this car and paced back towards the next one.

"Sir?" A woman said from behind him. "Are you the engineer?"

Kyrk stopped in his tracks and rolled his eyes. He spun around to see a helmeted, red-haired woman in her twenties with worn-out black boots and an equally worn-out reddish suit standing on the bridge.

"Car inspector, ma'am."

To his surprise, she darted back into the car. Moments later there came commotion from inside and even arguments. He walked back towards the door and shone his light inside. A young girl screamed from the back. "Don't let them take me!"

"What are you doing here?" Kyrk said.

No one responded. Instead they huddled together in fear.

"Oh, I get it. You guys are refugees of some sort. Look, I'm not a car inspector. I'm just looking for bullion."

"Why have we stopped?" Came a man's voice from the back in an angry tone.

"I think your engineer's taking a nap."

Goldman arrived at his side and stood in the doorway with his eyes wide open. He then turned to Kyrk. "This wasn't on the manifest was it?"

Kyrk focused on the woman who jumped out of the boxcar a minute ago. He shined his flashlight on her and noticed her holding a girl and a boy of about five years old under each arm. "Where are you folks from?"

The woman hesitated and looked around at the others. She then glared at Kyrk and said in a cold voice, "We're from the settlement near Pavonis Mons."

Kyrk looked back at Goldman. "Isn't that where the rebellion is going on? Near the mines?"

"When are we going to get moving again?" Another man in the back said. Soon, others in the crowd murmured.

"I'm sure your engineer will be back on his feet in no time." Kyrk looked down the track towards the platform. By now the sun was just over the horizon and everything around them reflected a reddish-orange hue.

Kyrk scampered towards the next boxcar and jerked the sliding door open. To his shock, he found this one full of machinery and in the back a dozen mining robots in hibernation. He ran back towards Goldman and motioned towards the side of the bridge. "We gotta bail."

"We can't just leave these people. What if they're prisoners? What if they're refugees and never make it?"

He stepped close to Goldman and whispered, "I learned a long time ago not to get involved in anybody's land wars."

Kyrk took off his backpack and undid the zipper on it. He pulled out a coil of rope and a harness and secured the harness around his waist. "We gotta go."

Before Goldman could react, Kyrk wrapped the other end of the coiled rope around one of the rails and put his backpack back on. He looked back to see Goldman sticking his head inside the car again.

Then came the sound in the distance towards the station that Kyrk did not want to hear. The engine powered back to life with a hum. Kyrk shouted back towards Goldman, "Now, Goldman!"

Goldman threw his own backpack onto the bridge and pulled out the harness and rope. He froze when the red-haired woman came back to the door of the boxcar.

"So that's it? You're going to leave us now? No offer to help us?"

"Where are you going?" Goldman asked her.

"The freelands. Go. Be on your way. Cowards." She headed back inside and began to tug the door shut.

At that Kyrk rappelled down from the bridge and estimated the desert floor to be some one hundred feet below him. He only had ninety feet of rope and winced at the thought of the final jump. Hopefully, he would not land on a patch of hard rock.

Goldman soon followed with his own rope and harness. A crunch sound travelled the length of the train as the engine came to life and motored forward.

Kyrk slid down the rope as fast as he could and Goldman soon caught up. The train cars rocked into motion and Kyrk could feel the vibration of the wheels rolling across his rope high above. Before he could react the rope slackened and he went into a freefall towards the sand below.

With a backward thud he punched the sand with his back and sent up a cloud of dust several feet into the air. Goldman soon followed.

He lay there motionless a few minutes while the train lumbered on across the trestle high above. He turned to look over at Goldman.

"You make it?"

Goldman raised his right hand and waved.

In the distance, Kyrk could see the sun on the horizon and to his left a series of jagged cliffs he had yet to explore.

"Goldman?"

Goldman raised his hand in the air again. "Still here."

"Ever get the feeling you've been set up?"

There was no reply.

"I wonder what happened to the guard at the outpost."

Again, no reply.

"Goldman?" Kyrk sat up. He felt a presence looming behind him and spun around. It was Goldman, who pointed a pistol at Kyrk's chest.

"I am the guard."

Kyrk slowly raised his hands into the air. "Hey now, take it easy."

"I heard about you. Did you really think it would be that easy to get access to all that bullion?"

"Yes."

"Get up."

Kyrk wrenched himself up from the grip of the soft sand, but stumbled as his knees tried to give out underneath him. He sunk a couple of inches into the sand and sensed he had no chance of breaking into a sprint. "What if I try to run?"

"You won't get far."

Kyrk tried to get into a better position to kick or punch the gun out of Goldman's hand.

"I wouldn't try that. You have three choices. You can run, I can turn you in, or you can make something useful of your life."

"And how would I choose option three?"

"Those people on the train. Who'd you think they were anyway?"

"Okay. I get it. You're helping them. They're refugees and you're going to make sure they make it to freedom. How much are they paying you for that?"

Goldman continued to point the gun at Kyrk's chest.

Kyrk lowered his hands. "Put the gun away, Goldman."

Goldman did nothing.

"Look. What do you see in an old guy like me anyway?"

"I have heard of you many times over the years. One of the best smugglers around these parts. Never caught but always gets the job done."

58

Kyrk smirked and studied his boots. He could use a new pair. "So you thought I would be good at smuggling people? That's a leap."

"Those people need you."

Goldman continued to point the gun at Kyrk, but lowered it to aim at Kyrk's feet. Looking at the gun, he wondered if Goldman was going to make him dance.

Kyrk put his hands on his hips and then picked up his backpack. "Goldman, you don't need to convince me. I think I saw my nephew in that first boxcar we opened."

IM Forever

In the afternoon Dr. Bellin awoke to an electrical storm with thunder so loud it nearly broke the hospital room's windows. He watched as bolt after bolt punched at the ground like white-hot rockets fired from on high.

He turned to his left to look over at the heart monitor at his bedside. Next to that was a rollaway table with an unopened crossword puzzle book, a plastic cup full of water, and a cell phone. He smiled weakly for if there was ever an optimum moment for his final experiment to commence it would be now.

He picked up the cell phone and cradled it's shiny, burnished crimson case in his arthritic hand. With a flip of his thumb the cover popped open and he rotated through his directory to find his colleague's number. After he dialed the number, a man's raspy voice answered.

"Hello?"

"Dr. Morbelli, I'm ready."

"Shall I notify your family?"

"After we're done."

A half-hour passed before Dr. Morbelli arrived. He wheeled in a machine on a cart, with a tangle of cables and electrodes on top and a television monitor next to that. He then rolled the cart next to the hospital bed and plugged the machine into a nearby electrical outlet. He untangled the spaghetti pile of cables and electrodes on top as a female nurse walked into the room.

"Are you sure this is safe?" The nurse asked, putting her hands on her hips.

"Yes, Amanda. Perfectly safe," said Dr. Bellin. "We've already tested it several times on myself and once on Jim, here."

"Okay, but I'm still unclear as to what you plan on doing with that machine."

Dr. Morbelli turned to face her. "It's simple. We hook up the electrodes and connect to the socket on the back of Dr. Bellin's head and upload all of his thoughts. Should take…about two to four hours."

"Two to four…hours?"

"That's fast," Dr. Bellin added. "I'll be calling my family when it's done."

The nurse left the room.

Dr. Bellin sat up and whispered to Dr. Morbelli, "She thinks we're both nuts."

"Outrageous. Doesn't she know we're on the cutting edge here? Good God, you started in your field as a pioneer and you're going out as one." Dr. Morbelli paused after that last comment and stared out the window. He then resumed untangling cables and draped several of them over the bed railing as if they were tentacles.

"You really feel the end is near?" He said, looking back at Dr. Bellin.

"I feel it. I can barely sit up anymore now. I can't dress myself anymore."

Dr. Morbelli strung the cables out from the black and silver computer sitting on top of the cart as if they were the arms of an octopus. He attached several cables to a wireframe helmet that looked more like a copper colander than a piece of scientific equipment. After a few adjustments he placed it on top of Dr. Bellin's head and plugged another cable into the socket at the back of his head.

Dr. Bellin turned once more towards the window and then back at the machine on the cart. He closed his eyes and nodded his head up and down.

With a twist of a knob and a few taps of the keyboard, Dr. Morbelli started the experiment. He stared on at the monitor a minute and then gave his assessment. "Fascinating."

Dr. Bellin smiled as he knew he had finally cheated death at last.

* * *

A day after the funeral of Dr. Bellin, Dr. Morbelli unplugged the hard drives from the bedside machine and plugged them into his desktop computer. The thought of transferring all of this data made him realize he would be the first person to fully clone a human mind.

He began to sort and organize the data the best he could, yet he knew it could be a process that would take years to complete if it could even be accomplished at all.

Some data came through as images and other bits of information came out as text. Some of the images appeared to be colored noise, while others looked like distorted scenes from childhood. Still others were full of meaningless bits of text, numbers, and even equations.

Their first attempt at transferring his thoughts looked better than this mess. A sense of depression washed over him now as he wondered if it was all a mistake.

Then, out of the screens and screens of data, a pattern appeared. He noticed what appeared to be data likely related to short term memory and other data sets related to long term. There were pictures of the laboratory from several months ago and others of a birthday party held at Dr. Bellin's bedside.

Then came whiteboards full of equations he had never seen. Drawings of electronic devices imagined yet never realized on paper. Fragments of fantastic designs dreamt but never spoken of. After that came pictures of weapons yet to be built. Horrific and haunting, they caused him to stare at the screen for minutes at a time.

The telephone rang, shattering his concentration and the silence of the laboratory. He looked at the identification display on the phone. It was another friend, Dr. Corwin.

"Have you had a chance to look over the data yet?" Dr. Corwin said.

"It's amazing. He had ideas for dozens of devices. Medical devices, communication devices, weapons…"

"You're not thinking of publishing those, are you?"

"I'm publishing all of it. Those were his wishes."

"Not the weapons. What if they cause great harm?"

"Tom, it's all going online. I think it'll all work itself out. If all these ideas lead us forward…"

"It's irresponsible of you. And him. Think about what you're doing, Jim. Have you gone through the data yet?"

"No. I will, but I'll need help."

"Have you hired any staff to help?"

"I don't need staff. I've got the world. Hundreds, maybe thousands can help us sort the data."

"Have you been listening to anything I've been saying? Jim, we all know this guy was a genius, but he had a dark side to his…"

"Good day, Tom."

Dr. Morbelli hung up the phone and sorted through some random images of cars, people, and equations. Then he checked on his server connection.

With the press of a key, he started the upload.

* * *

Six months later, Dr. Morbelli walked out of his lab one night and was greeted by a bearded man in his early twenties, wearing a green camouflage jacket and torn blue jeans. The man approached the doctor as he walked towards his car. In the man's hands was a box-shaped device that reflected the moonlight.

"Dr. Morbelli?" The man extended his hand to shake.

The doctor held out his hand, but withdrew it quickly. "Can I help you?"

"You already have. What you and Dr. Bellin did was incredible. Just incredible."

The man held the shiny box under his left arm and swung his other arm wildly in the air. The man stared straight at Dr. Morbelli with an intensity that caused him to sweat.

Dr. Morbelli nodded but crept towards his car. The man cut him off.

"You've got to see what I've done. Here." The man set the device on the sidewalk. "Know what this does? Do you recognize the plan?"

He lied. "I…I'm sorry. I don't."

"It's a quantum scatter box. This bugger can blow away small objects with a button press. Rocks, cars, trucks. I bet this thing could take out a whole house."

Dr. Morbelli crept towards his car. "Thanks for sharing, but I really need to get going."

"Watch. I'm gonna demo it for you."

"There's no directional array on it."

"A directional what? Here, let me show you."

Dr. Morbelli then ran to his car. He ducked inside and saw the man reaching down towards the machine. In a second, he started his car and roared out of the parking lot. In his rear view mirror he saw the box glow bright green and then a bright flash of light filled his field of vision. A spruce tree near the laboratory building lit up like a Christmas tree and disappeared in a wisp of smoke.

At that, he pulled over to the side of the road. The box lit up again with a bright green glow. Dr. Morbelli scrambled out of his car and opened the rear door on the driver's side. He reached into the back seat and pulled out a cardboard box.

He set the box on the ground and lifted out the Bellin quantum scatter shield and reflector. After a few adjustments, he set the device on the pavement and unfolded its metallic foil wings into the shape of a dish. With a simple turn, he aimed the dish towards the intensifying glow of the scatter box.

Another flash lit up the laboratory parking lot but this time no trees were vaporized. Instead the quantum scatter box itself went up in a mushroom cloud of white, glittering smoke.

"You seem to have forgotten something," Dr. Morbelli called out to the man, who now stood bewildered on the sidewalk. His hands trembled along with his voice as he reached down to adjust the shield. "It helps to read *all* of the instructions first."

A Moveable Peace

The hallways of the Rigel Spacefleet Academy were supposed to be passageways between classes and not tests of endurance. For Ben Melendez each day in the hallways featured several races between doors and honed his avoidance skills if nothing else.

"Hey rook," said a voice from behind him. Ben had almost made it out of the cafeteria and past the game room when he felt a not-so-subtle tap on his left shoulder. To turn around meant certain confrontation and to walk away meant an even bigger confrontation next hour.

"Rook, turn around, I'm talking to you."

Ben spun around on one heel and clutched his textbook tight. He hoped it did not have to double as a weapon. In front of him stood Robbie, a fellow classmate with a brash attitude and a mouth that got him into more trouble than his fists. On either side of him were two friends, one short and skinny and the other tall and muscular, who flanked him like wingmen on a mission from Misery Incorporated.

Robbie strolled up to Ben and jabbed a thick finger into his chest. "I challenge you to a game in the crucible."

"What's that?"

"You really are a rook, aren't you?" Robbie grinned at his pals and grabbed a handful of Ben's shirt. He dragged Ben by the shirt towards the game room until Ben snapped himself free.

Ben stared on at the slate-blue machine in the corner that was ten feet across and six feet high. It sat on the floor like a giant windowless shoebox with a sliding door on the front. The sides of the machine were covered in comic-book-like artwork with two characters hurling fireballs at each other. Above those figures was a banner that read "Pyrocyclotron".

He watched two other recruits exit the simulator, laughing as if they had just seen a comedic movie. To Ben, it was a joke that he had to spend his time calculating the fastest path to the exit.

"What do you say we up the stakes a little?" Robbie said, with a sneer in his voice. "If you win, I'll give you a day's worth of my store credits. If I win, I get half your meal credits for a week, your store credits for a day, and you get my kitchen duties for a week."

"I'm not agreeing to that. That's not fair."

"You're right. If I win, I should get a week's worth of your store credits."

At this point, Ben felt another one of the recruits bury an elbow in his back. He gasped for air and lurched towards the simulator. Robbie's other friend stood in the game room doorway like a self-appointed guard.

"I take that as a yes. You first," Robbie barked as he shoved Ben towards the sliding door and attempted to trip him in the process.

Ben dove inside of the simulator and found himself standing before a square, smoked-glass table with two black metal chairs on opposite sides. On the table was a glass board, fifty by fifty squares, with two grooved trays on either side of the board. Inside of the trays were neon blue and ruby red glass discs and above the table was a lamp that illuminated the entire setup.

Ben pulled out a chair and sat down opposite Robbie at the table. He turned back to look at the sliding door to see several of Robbie's friends grinning. One of them slammed the door shut with a laugh.

Robbie leaned back in his chair and looked at Ben as if he felt sorry for him. That look was soon swept away by an acid grin. "You first, rook."

"What do I do?"

"You put the discs on the board." Robbie pointed to a chart on the wall next to them. "You get points for every pattern you make. Once you make enough patterns you win. Got it, genius?"

Ben studied the chart on the wall just long enough to memorize the patterns. He withdrew a neon blue disc from the grooved tray in front of him and placed it onto the center of the board.

The room suddenly went black and the glass board before him lit up into a grid-like pattern of crisscrossing glowing white lines. His disc glowed neon blue, as did all of the discs in his tray. The ruby red discs in Robbie's tray also glowed and Robbie then placed his disc adjacent to Ben's first move.

The wall behind Robbie suddenly exploded to life with a faint crimson aura. Ben turned around and looked at the wall behind him. It, too, glowed with a faint aura, but his was a pale blue. An eerie light was thrown on their hands and faces and when he turned back Robbie was irritated.

"I don't have all day."

Ben tried to look at the chart on the wall, but he found it difficult to see the patterns. Instead, he reasoned, he would have to go off of his memory. He placed another disc diagonally adjacent to his first move in order to start building a five-in-a-row combination.

Robbie's next move cut him off. No sounds came from the shifting curtain of light behind him, but the display suddenly changed.

The wall behind Robbie sprang to life with images of an Indian market, full of street vendors, customers, fruit stands, and colorful textile vendors as far as the eye could see. Seconds later explosions erupted as a column of tanks roared into the village. The tanks rolled into the market, crushing the stands and sending people scattering in panic. Then, the turrets began to open fire. Hot white and orange flashes lit up the screen as the tanks fired and shells punched their way through the market and into nearby buildings.

Ben refocused his eyes on the game. He felt drops of sweat forming on the back of his neck and noticed Robbie seemed to get some type of warped enjoyment out of the situation. Disc after disc was put onto the board until Robbie pulled off a five-in-a-row move.

Suddenly, a digitized scoreboard came to life on the wall where the chart was supposed to be. Ben worked out several board moves in his head and started to build a new strategy on the fly.

Robbie became agitated and annoyed by the new moves and appeared distracted by something on the screen behind Ben. Minutes later his face turned sour as Ben pulled off a rare small "x" maneuver.

The scoreboard lit up on Ben's side. The victory felt brief because the screen behind Robbie changed to an image of a couple holding hands and walking down the street at night. The couple paused to look in a shop window.

They suddenly looked towards the sky and then fled in terror as planes roared overhead and firebombed the city. Image after image showed flames devouring businesses, cars, and even homes.

As the battle on the board raged on, the scoreboard on the wall reflected the alternating nature of the conflict. Ben did his best to hide his thought processes but Robbie's eyes burned with a bottled rage that could incinerate the table.

Then the images behind Robbie darkened even further. Instead of a village or a downtown street, an image of a deer grazing in a sunlit meadow appeared. This time, however, the deer looked up and soon a mushroom cloud went off. A blizzard of flame swept away the meadow and the birch trees behind it. Homes imploded. Cars overturned. Radio towers fell and the forest convulsed under the onslaught of heat and wind. There was no time to run.

Ben counted the discs left in his tray. There were only four moves left and the score was tied. His mind raced through the possibilities as his stomach rolled. He spotted a place for a large "x" but then there would be missed blocks in another corner of the board. In another place he could nail a five-in-a-row, but then he would succumb to missed blocks elsewhere.

Then, suddenly, he viewed the board in a new way. A triple score opened up and at that point the missed blocks would not matter. He set his blue glass disc in place and watched as Robbie's glare intensified. The screen behind him filled with a series of frenetic images of war, revenge, and confusion. The scoreboard lit up and declared Ben the winner.

Robbie stood up. He pounded his fist on the table and knocked a handful of pieces to the floor. He swept his right hand across the board and knocked the rest of the discs against the wall.

The room lights came up and Ben dove for the door handle. Before Robbie could catch him he slid the door open and burst outside. Behind him he could hear the conversations of the other recruits.

Robbie stormed out a second later. He yelled out to Ben, "Hey! What was that?"

By this point, Ben was already halfway down the hallway adjacent to the game room. He turned back to see a bewildered yet angry Robbie with his hands on his hips standing next to the simulator.

"What are you talking about?"

"On the screen. Behind you. It was up there the whole time. Like a rock or something."

Ben looked at the floor then back up at Robbie. A broad smile broke across his face. "A Rock, huh? That was no ordinary Rock."

Ben shuffled forward a few feet and then stopped. "Oh and by the way, the store is down this way."

The View From Under the Bridge

Dennis pored over the last, long, folding table at the garage sale and turned to walk away. As he headed down the driveway, a shoebox of gray plastic cartridges commanded his attention.

He peered into the box and found ten featureless cartridges with rows of gold pin connectors on one end. He picked one up out of the box and flipped it over in his hands. Without hesitating he put the cartridge back, scooped the box up under one arm, and approached the makeshift cash register.

The white-haired woman behind the card table with the cash box stood up to greet him. "Did you find what you were looking for?"

"These should keep me busy for a while." He set the shoebox on the table and held out some cash.

"I'm glad you can make use of them. My husband and I found them on a hiking trip. It looked like someone just dumped them in the middle of the woods. We picked 'em up, cleaned 'em off, but didn't know what to do with 'em. What are they anyway?"

"They're android cartridges. You plug them into a robot's processor brain. They're from the A6-12 line but I can get them up and running."

She took his cash and handed him back some change. He picked up the shoebox and left.

* * *

Dennis sat in the workshop and picked up one of the gray cartridges. He plugged it into the back of a test android's head. It stuck out at a funny angle but it was the best he could do since he had to rig up an adapter on the fly. The android was an A8-1, with more advanced processors than an A6-12 model, and better power regeneration circuits.

"Let's see what you got." He looked into the robot's glass eyes and fired up the machine. The eyes immediately lit up with a faint blue aura.

The android turned its head to face Dennis. "Where am I?"

"You're in a workshop. What's your name?"

"Tony Collins."

Dennis picked up on something cold, almost calculating in the way the name was said. "Tell me about yourself."

"Why? Who are you? Where am I again? My head feels funny." The android lifted his hand and attempted to scratch the back of its head.

"Please don't do that."

"Do you have a light?"

"What would you need that for? I have a flashlight over here."

"Not a flashlight. A light. A smoke." The android again attempted to scratch its head but Dennis reached out to block the android's arm with his hand. His hand was swatted away.

"I told you, something doesn't feel right. My head hurts." The android bent over in its chair and put both hands on the sides of its head.

"Androids don't smoke."

"What? Look, the last thing I remember was being in a lab room of some sort. Like a doctor's office. People are asking me questions. Non-stop questions. Tell me about your childhood. What was Dad like? I don't know. He was always at the bar. On and on. Now I'm in another room. Same questions, same answers. Don't you people write anything down? Where's Hogan? Never..."

Dennis unplugged the cartridge from the android's head. He wrote on a white label the words "Tony Collins" and attached it to the cartridge. He then set it into another shoebox on the workbench. He pulled out a second gray cartridge and plugged it into the back of the android's head.

It took a minute for the machine to respond and lift up its head. This time the voice was female and the android stared at Dennis a moment before slowly turning away.

"Oh, what do you want?" She said. The android looked at its hands and legs, then over at Dennis again. "What is this? Where are my hands and legs? You're not Dr. Hogan."

"No, I'm Dennis."

The android stood up. "Where's Dr. Hogan? I'm confused. I need to get the laundry done."

"Hogan? Who is that?" Dennis drew back and studied her eyes intently. He braced himself for any sudden movements on the android's part.

"Dr. Hogan. Lambert Hogan." The android stood up and began to pace around the room. "The laundry. The kids are coming home soon. I have to get the laundry done."

Dennis sprang up out of his chair and lunged for the cartridge. With a jerk, he unplugged it and then walked it over to a nearby workbench.

The android's arms went limp. The legs kept it upright, which was a failsafe reaction on these models, as it stared blankly across the room. The eyes, as usual, were dark with their color drained completely.

Dennis printed the name "Lucy" on the cartridge label. He walked over to a laptop computer on the neighboring workbench and attempted to search for the "Dr. Lambert Hogan".

After minutes of searching, he came across a match—the web page of a local university professor whose research areas included robotics and network communications. He picked up the phone and dialed the number on the screen. The number was disconnected.

He pulled another cartridge out of the garage-sale shoebox and walked over to the android. With one push he plugged in the cartridge and waited.

The machine straightened up, surveyed its surroundings, walked back over to the wooden chair where Dennis originally put it, and sat down. This time, the android kept its arms at its sides and turned to face Dennis. Dennis pulled out another label and held the pen above it like a hammer readied to strike.

"Taking notes?" The android said in a male voice.

"Not quite. Do you know where you are?"

The android panned around the room. "In a laboratory."

"Have you heard of a Dr. Lambert Hogan?"

The android looked to the side then back up at Dennis. "Can't say that I have. If I may ask, what am I doing here?"

Dennis leaned back, amused. "I found you in a shoebox."

"How did I get there?"

"That's my question. It's my understanding someone dumped you and your friends off in the woods."

The android continued to stare straight ahead.

"Did you know Dr. Hogan?" Dennis asked again.

"Never heard of him."

Dennis continued to pepper the android with questions. At the end of the conversation, he put the unit into hibernation mode, left the workshop, and went inside the house.

* * *

In the morning, Dennis arose early and headed over to the workshop. He froze on the back steps of the house when he found the door of the workshop had been left open. Upon closer inspection, he noticed no signs of visible entry to the workshop or the nearby garage.

He darted into the workshop to find it dark. He flipped on the lights and paced around the room, but noticed nothing appeared to be missing. Then he turned to look towards the doorway.

The wooden chair where the A8-1 model sat last night was empty.

He raced back out into the backyard. The front fence gate was ajar, but again there were no signs of destructive entry. Dennis locked up the workshop and ran back into the house. He scooped up the conference flyer he printed out the night before and marched toward the front door.

* * *

Dennis walked up to the hotel parking lot and looked around. It was a long shot at best, but without a tracking device on the android it was the best choice he could think of. He paced slowly up to the hotel entrance and stepped inside.

In the hotel lobby several conference attendees mingled, sipped coffee, and pored over folding tables loaded down with sign-up forms, brochures, books, and videos. He dodged a woman sitting at one of the tables who appeared to be in charge of registration.

He stepped into the auditorium where he could hear someone speaking and checked a brochure he picked up off one of the tables.

Dennis stared at the speaker, who, according to the speaking schedule in the brochure, was Dr. Lambert Hogan. He then scanned the crowd.

Up above and behind Dr. Hogan on a screen was a slide that contained a diagram about transferring human thoughts into machine brains. Out of the corner of his eye and to his left he saw someone lifting their arms up as if to point.

It was the A8-1 android.

Dennis bolted immediately towards the machine and tackled it to the ground. In the android's hands he found a pistol. Dennis knocked the pistol out of his hands and grasped the cartridge in back of the android's head.

All around him he heard gasps, which then turned to alarm and confusion. Dr. Lambert stopped his speech and by the time Dennis unplugged the cartridge he could hear people closing in around him.

Dennis stuffed the cartridge in his pocket and stood up to face Dr. Hogan. "Why don't you tell them about what you really do? Who are you experimenting on?"

He immediately felt hands grabbing at him as another man stepped in between him and the stage. Dennis pulled away from them and began to drag the android out of the room by the arms.

Over the loudspeaker, he could hear Dr. Hogan making some comments about crazed and deranged protestors. Dennis turned around and shot back, "I'm not crazed and deranged."

Another man in a blue suit kept pushing him towards the door. "Get out of here. You'll be lucky if we don't press charges."

Dennis pushed his way back outside, still dragging the dead weight of the inanimate android behind him. As if to follow him all the way out to the parking lot, he heard shuffling and shouting behind him coming from the hotel lobby.

He dragged the android down the sidewalk for several blocks until he found a wooden park bench. He sat the machine down on the bench and wedged the robot's hands between the back part of the bench and the seat to hold them in place.

He fished the cartridge out of his pocket and plugged it back into the android's head. There was a moment of hesitation before the machine attempted to move.

"Good morning. My name is Dennis. I'm here to help you. I know where Dr. Hogan is. Tell me all you know about him."

The android immediately tried to struggle and break itself free from the bench. "Why should I?"

Dennis sat down next to the android as if waiting for a city bus. "My family says they found me abandoned one night while driving through the city. They picked me up, brought me home, and restored my circuits."

"So?"

"So...I'm an android, too."

* * *

That night, around one in the morning, Dennis strolled on a paved walking path near a bridge that crossed over the Mississippi River. On the road that ran alongside the path he heard a vehicle approach from behind but did not see any light being cast from the vehicle's headlights. He heard the engine stop and two car doors slam shut.

Without looking back he continued to walk until he heard a rustle behind him. Suddenly, someone threw a black hood or bag over his head. In an instant his arms were wrenched behind his back. Something struck the side of his head but being an android the blow did not knock him out.

He felt himself being dragged through the grass and was lifted into a vehicle. In his right hand he clutched a brown paper bag with a liquor bottle inside. With a hard shove he was thrown into the back of the vehicle, which he determined to likely be a van.

Two doors slammed shut. Then, two other doors opened and were shut.

"Man, that one was heavy for his size," said a male voice from behind him.

"What did you expect? I told you he was going to be dead weight," said another male voice.

Dennis analyzed the second voice. It was Dr. Hogan. Tonight, it seemed he was travelling with an unknown companion doing what they had done before: making rounds to the areas where the homeless wandered, only to snatch them off the street, stuff them in a van, and bring them back to the lab for research.

Dennis continued to listen for a few minutes and felt the vehicle lurch forward and then accelerate. After a few minutes, it came to a stop. He spoke up when the moment was right.

"I need to go to the bathroom."

"What?" The first male voice said.

"I said I need to go to the bathroom."

The two men in the front of the van swore and argued with each other. The vehicle lurched forward again, and then stopped hard. A door opened. Dennis set down the bottle and the bag he was carrying and tripped a switch on the top of the bottle. Another door opened and Dennis felt a tangle of angry arms grab him by the pant legs and drag him out of the vehicle.

"Get out. And hurry it up," said a dark, agitated voice.

The hood came off Dennis' head. In the dark he found himself closer to the River bridge and on the riverbank.

A second man behind him mumbled, "I thought you said this was a man. Looks like an android to me."

"An android?" It was Dr. Hogan's voice again. "Hey, is that the one who was at the conference? Kill it."

Suddenly, Dennis felt a sharp blow to the back of his head, but this one knocked him off his feet. It temporarily scrambled his neurological circuits and shut down his vision for a few seconds.

When his retinal circuits recovered, he found himself flat on his side and staring up towards the bridge deck. His arm and leg motors refused to fire but he was able to pivot his head slightly. Out of the corner of his eye he saw the black van pull off and roll towards the bridge.

In the fading light of his electronic retinas he watched as the van began to cross onto the bridge. Soon an explosion could be heard in the back of the van and it swerved to stay on the road. After several attempts to regain control the van plummeted off the bridge and into the river below.

A ball of flame erupted, followed by a spectacular splash. As his electronic retinal receptors faded to black, Dennis felt his systems shut down one after the other. One final thought circuited his brain and came to his lips: "The laundry. The kids are coming home soon. I have to get the laundry done. The laundry. The kids are coming home soon..."

Cities of the Plain

The three of them climbed up the grassy hill under a cloudless sky. The afternoon sun was warm, but not intense, and as they descended down the other side of the hill the shore of the Dead Sea came into view. Isaiah followed some ten feet behind his father and mother and carried a fishing net, a green plastic pail full of toys, and a green plastic shovel. He caught up to his father and tugged on his father's shirt.

"Are we almost there?"

"Almost. Only another couple hundred feet or so."

Isaiah fell behind again and listened as his father discussed the area.

"Can you believe it, Charlotte? They said this region was once overrun with armies. Dropped like flies as they moved in for the attack."

Isaiah looked around on the ground for signs of a battle but found none. He tuned out his father again and as they descended he caught sight of a curving beach full of sand that had a few rocks on it, an occasional palm tree, but little else. He ran ahead and called out to his parents.

"Here?"

"Yes. Here is good," his father said. "We'll be down the shore a bit." His father pointed to the left. He grabbed the fishing net from his son and turned towards a rocky outcropping next to the beach.

"What's this place called?"

"En Gedi. It's called En Gedi."

* * *

An hour passed. Isaiah continued to play in the sand, digging roads and tunnels before settling on a plan to build a city full of sand castles. He watched his parents pull in fish after fish. He saw his father wade out into the water with his pant legs rolled up and dip the fishing net into the deep several times.

In front of him, sand mound after sand mound turned into a castle and one even turned into a three-story apartment building. He poked holes in the sides of the mounds with a stick to create windows. Roads flowed in and around the buildings as he pushed his die-cast metal cars in circuits around them.

Behind him he heard the squawk of a bird, and when he turned to look it flew off of the perch it was on and soared out over the sea. He stood up and brushed the sand off of his dark blue shorts. He walked over to where the bird once perched because it looked like a small rock that he could use in his city.

The rock turned out to be a pointed cylinder lying on its side, half buried in the sand. He pushed at it with his bare foot, but it did not budge. With a sharp jerk of his hands he pulled it free from the wet sand and dragged it back to his sand castle city.

Isaiah put the metal object on the edge of his city and built up the sand around its base. This new rocket of a skyscraper loomed above his apartment building and cast a shadow over some of the highways he had carved out of the sand.

Suddenly, he heard the sound of his father's voice and looked up. His father approached carrying a thick stick across both shoulders. On each end of the stick hung a white bucket, surely full of fish.

"Come on Isaiah, it's time to go. We've got dinner."

"In a minute."

Isaiah pushed a green car around the rocket skyscraper and parked it. He then started on a house. As he shaped and sculpted the smooth, wet sand between his fingertips, he heard his mother's voice call out. Pretending not to hear, he squared off the roof with his green shovel.

"C'mon, Isaiah. This load is heavy," she said.

Isaiah finished off the roof and poked several holes in the new building for windows. He sat and admired his creation a moment. He heard his parents approach and stood up.

"Isaiah, what is that?" His mother came up to the edge of his city as he looked around for his cars, shovel, and bucket.

"Here, pick this all up." She stuffed the toys in his bucket and led him towards his waiting father.

"Jim, come here a second. What do make of this?"

Jim set the stick and the buckets of fish down onto the sand. He marched over to stand next to Charlotte as Isaiah stood back and watched them both.

"Isaiah, where'd you find this? Tell me." His dad scolded him.

"It was…it was over there." He pointed down the beach.

"What do you make of it?" His mother said again.

"Looks like a mortar. C'mon, let's go."

"Can I take it with?" Isaiah asked, still holding his bucket of toys.

"No," his father snapped. He walked over and grabbed Isaiah by the hand. "We have to leave those things behind. Next time you see one of those, don't touch it. You hear me?"

Isaiah shook his head but turned back to look at his sand castle city and the rocket skyscraper that stood proudly above everything else.

"I thought you said they cleared the beaches of this," his mother said.

"Charlotte, let's not talk about these things anymore."

About the Author

Michael Galloway is an outdoors enthusiast whose interests include camping, fishing, hiking, writing, and technology. He has a degree in Journalism, and has been writing software in one language or another for over twenty years. He currently lives in Minnesota with his family.

* * *

Also by Michael Galloway

An Echo Through the Trees
Theft at the Speed of Light
Horizons
Gathering the Wind
Fractal Standard Time